I promise to write in this book and get it dirty, to press leaves in it, draw in it, collect dirt samples in it, decorate it and use it in whatever manner I see fit (but NOT if it's a library book--that's just rude).

_____
(Sign Name)

Congratulations! You are now a GeEk!

Thank you times ten to my Team, Marie and Lisa, who helped make the story and made it make sense, and Kathleen, my special nature friend and mentor.

To my daughter, Jen, who went with me on this island adventure and to Kenny and Goober.

For Kyah!

This book is totally Michigan-made!

Library of Congress Cataloging-in-Publication Data
Taylor, Lori
Holly Wild: Bamboozled on Beaver Island—1st U.S. Edition
Third Printing, Feb. 2015
Summary: Holly Wild dreams of following in the footsteps of her famed explorer relatives. When she visits Beaver Island with her friends for Museum Week activities, the kids find themselves faced with wildlife, villains, and unruly monsters.

ISBN 978-1-4507-9194-6
[1. Nature—fiction. 2. Snakes—fiction. 3. Beaver Island—fiction.
4. Science—fiction.]
Library of Congress Control Number: 2011937401

Published in the U.S.A., September 2011
by Bear Track Press, Pinckney, MI
Printed in the U.S.A. by Greko Printing, Plymouth, MI

www.loritaylorart.com

HOLLY WILD:

Bamboozled on BEAVER ISLAND

By
Lori Taylor

Bear Track Press
Pinckney, MI

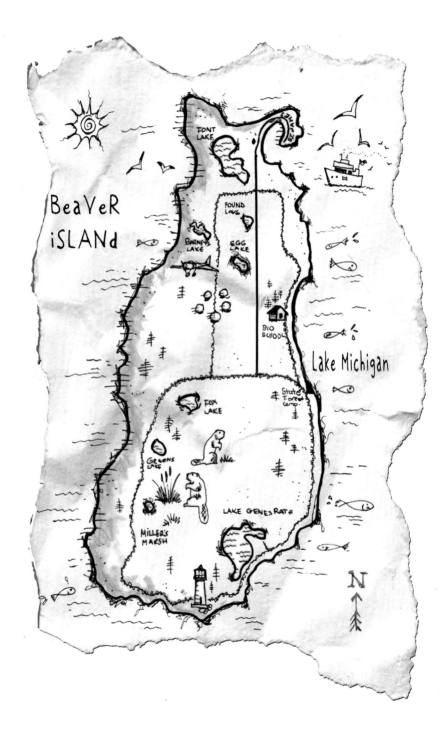

When I fell, my hands had instinctively flown out and grabbed onto the snout of the yellow-eyed beast. This was a good thing--I was holding its jaws shut. I wondered if this was what it was like when Great Aunt Daisy Crockett leaped onto the bear for her brother.

Chapter 1
Into the Wilds

Nothing but toes and a tail dangled from his mouth. Holy creeps! If I, Holly H. Wild, were going to win, I'd have to hurry.

I peered through the glass watching and wishing that I could open my jaws that wide. I crammed the rest of the PBJ into my mouth. I was still swallowing my sandwich when the rat's tail disappeared. Kenny, my new pet corn snake, won. I blamed my loss on peanut butter.

"Nexth time," I said, the peanut butter bread glue ball stuck to the roof of my mouth. I jotted down the date and what Kenny ate in my notebook. I gulped some milk to push the PBJ lump down. Kenny yawned and smiled. His lunch lump was moving, too.

Kenny's a redhead like me. He's a candy corn snake, all orangey-red like the Halloween candy—only four feet longer. Gram brought him home two weeks ago, the same day my best friends, Tierra and Sierra, left for Florida. He's my first pet and I get to take care of him. For now, Mom says he has to live in Gram's room—she's afraid he'll get lost in mine.

Kenny and I ate lunch early today so I could go see Tierra and Sierra. They got back from their vacation last night and Mom said I had to wait until noon to go over. Something about going over too early would be rude. Anyway, the clock on the wall seemed like it was stuck on 11:50 for forever, so I climbed on a chair to check the batteries. That's when Gram came clomping into the house, yelling.

"Eureka! Fabulous news!" She was hollering and waving a letter over her head like a flag.

the adventure begins

"Mother Wild!" groaned Mom, emerging from the basement with a load of wet laundry. "Remember to wipe your feet. I just mopped!"

"Sorry, dear," Gram said, wiping her hiking boots on the carpet. Gram's like me—we're good at forgetting.

"What's your news, Gram?" I asked, my eagle eye scanning the yellow envelope she held. There was a drawing of a frowning cat sitting in a patch of flowers on it.

"This family needs a change," Gram said, winking at me.

"No more changes! This is the fourth load of laundry today," Mom said, plopping the basket of wet laundry and clothespins onto the chair next to me.

"Not change, like clothes. Change, as in scenery. This family needs a vacation. We've all been invited to visit your Aunt Kitty. You finally get to meet her, Holly."

"Whah? Huh?" Boy, my big brother, mumbled from the den. He was still in video game stupor mode. Since school let out he did nothing but play games.

"We could all use some fresh air and sunshine. So we're going to Beaver Island for Museum Week. Kitty's lecturing on flowers and snakes, and there's a pet show, an art show, music, and sandy beaches. It'll be fun! Holly can bring her friends."

"Wait a minute," Mom said. "Beaver Island? We're going to an island of beavers? Beavers aren't very artistic, nor do they make very good pets. In fact, they're messy and muddy."

"Snakes, beavers, museums! Awesome, times ten!" I said as I jumped down, knocking over my glass. The milky river rushed toward the clean laundry and Mom raced after it with a pair of Boy's boxer shorts. The milk won.

"Music! Beaches!" Boy croaked, turning away from his game. Other than his friends, music and video games were his life.

"Reading, rest and relaxation!" Mom said, wringing the milk out of Boy's boxer shorts over the sink full of dirty dishes.

"Tierra and Sierra will like the art show. I don't know what Beaver Island is, but it sounds really wild," I said.

"Ah, Beaver Island. That place never changes. I just love how unspoiled and unhurried it is there. Some of our Wild relatives even came from there," Gram said.

"When do we leave, Gram?" I asked, pulling my hat down. I, Holly H. Wild, was ready for adventure. Coming from a long line of Wild women wrasslers, wranglers and wanderers, this was my big chance for discovery and perhaps fame.

"Oh, didn't I say? Tomorrow. We leave tomorrow! Kitty's lectures start Monday," said Gram.

"Tomorrow?" Mom slumped down on to a pair of milk-soaked socks, then jumped back up. Poor Mom. Now she had wet shorts, too. Gram was right, Mom needed a change. We all needed a change.

"I need to get us ready!" Mom said, grabbing the milky laundry basket and heading back into the basement.

"Holy creeps!" I jumped up. "I gotta go tell Tierra and Sierra. Museums, beavers and snakes! Snakes?" I said, running into the sliding glass door. *BAM!*

Right then I remembered Kenny.

Chapter 2
Wild Secrets

"Hey, Gram, can I enter Kenny in the pet show?" I asked, rubbing my head.

"Oh, Holly," Gram sighed, laying down Aunt Kitty's letter. "Even though Kenny is the prettiest, sweetest, most talented climbing snake around, he's over four feet long. We just don't have room to take his tank. Sorry, sweetie, he'll have to sit this one out."

"But who'll take care of him while we're gone? Dad's scared of snakes."

"You just fed him, that'll hold him 'til we get back. He'll be fine," Gram said, reaching past the frozen rats in the freezer to get the ice cream.

I picked up the envelope to examine the drawings. Tiny blue pressed flowers fluttered out. "Hey, Gram. Why did Aunt Kitty draw a sad cat on the envelope? Did her cat die?"

"No, Holly," said Gram, eating straight from the carton. "Kitty has always signed her letters with

a cat drawing. Kitty's sad because there's trouble brewing on

Beaver Island. Big changes. But it can't be too dangerous if she's inviting us there, right?" Gram licked the spoon and winked at me.

"Awesome, times three! A vacation, adventure, *and* a mystery! I can't wait to meet Aunt Kitty," I said, imagining a much younger Gram. Someone big, tough and rugged like the other Wild women I'd always heard about. The vacation invitation must be Aunt Kitty's way of asking for our Wild help.

"Your Aunt Kitty was named after your Great-Great-Great Aunt Daisy Crockett," Gram said. "Wild Cat Crockett they called her."

DAISY WILD
"Wild Cat"

PAULINE BUNYAN

Wranglers

Wrasslers

Wanderers

JENNY APPLESEED

WILD WOMEN

Of all the Wilds, from Cousin Pauline Bunyan from the Upper Peninsula, to Aunt Jenny Appleseed, it was Daisy Crockett Wild who was talked about most. The little sister of Davy, she saved his life once by wrestling a bear. But History books don't much like talking about a little girl of eight rescuing her big, strong brother.

"Gotta get packin'," Gram said as she left the kitchen, leaving the ice cream sitting on the table.

Now it's my turn to become a Wild legend! I pulled my tan hat down and ran to lay out my new, old explorer daypack from Gram. Ever since the day that Gram pulled it down from her closet shelf in a shower of insect skeletons and spider legs, I knew I was destined to put it to good use. It had been her exploring pack and she had passed it down to me. It even came with a lucky wildcat tail that had belonged to Daisy. I inhaled its smells of pine forest and campfire smoke, mixed with a touch of mildew. It was roomy and strong, and after years of being coated with bug spray and crusted with pancake batter it was pretty much waterproof. This

NEW, old daypack
Holds 50 pounds of gear, wet and dry, food, socks, rocks and important stuff.

Decorated with buttons and pins

● piney smell
● mildewish

● spider legs & beetley bodies
● pancake batter
● bug spray
● miscellaneous grime
● grape jelly stains

"bear bells"

would be my first real expedition to take it on.

When I strapped on the pack my brain started tingling and

my toes started wiggling. I felt dizzy, yet super-energized. Then I remembered Gram called that feeling wanderlust. She said every Wild woman gets it. It gives you itchy feet—which is different from Boy's athlete's foot, which is gross. Gram says itchy feet means you want to get out and see the world.

Every event in our Wild family history has led up to this moment. Right now, I would begin to live up to my Wild roots and become famous. Right now, I would begin my career as an explorer. Right now, I had to go tell Tierra and Sierra!

Running out the door, I tumbled down the front steps. When I bounced back up I realized that the backpack even made me invincible to pain. Awesome!

Getting to Sierra and Tierra Hills' house is no easy task. First, I have to pass through our neighbor's yard, the evil Buckthorns, without being accosted by their yapping poodle. Then, I have to get past Ivy Buckthorn herself, Arch Enemy Number One, without *her* yapping at me.

The Buckthorns are the down side of living in the town of Hayfields. Mr. Buckthorn is a builder and likes everything big. Big

Bowling ball shrubs + golf course grass + stick tree - flowers = BORING!

"Buckthorn Manor"

(Bonus points for vultures overhead.)

GET UP

house, big car, big money. And as luck would have it, their big, boring white house, which sits in the middle of their big, boring yard with one sickly stick tree, stands between my friends' house and mine—like a big, ripe pimple. But that's OK. I get to practice sneak and stalk mode, a technique for watching wildlife, every time I go to the Hills' house.

My best friends, Sierra (or Sie, pronounced like "sea") and Tierra (or T), are twins, but don't look or act alike. Both have brown hair and brown eyes, but they couldn't be any more different. Sie is a quiet, weather geek/ photographer who embraces an urban cowboy/bookworm look. T is an artsy, social butterfly/animal nut/math geek. But when they're standing next to each other and I cross my eyes, they blend into one strange, combined person. It can be fun, unless they're angry with me—then the doubly angry thing makes me squirm. But, I try not to let that happen —too much.

We met in second grade. It was my first day of school at Hayfields

Elementary. For show and tell, I handed my teacher a rare bird's nest I found in the road on the way to the bus stop. Much to my surprise it turned out not to be a nest at all, but a "road apple," more commonly known as horse manure.

Ivy Buckthorn bellowed "Horse poop!" Everyone in the class laughed—everyone but Sierra and Tierra. At recess they studied the "nest" with me. Sie examined the different grains the horse had eaten and T admired its artistic texture. Right then we became Team Wild. And right then we became GeEKs.

Not "geek" geeks, although we are an unusual bunch, but GeEKs, as in Geo-Explorer Kids. It's our own secret club and our mission is to learn about and protect nature. Right now it's just us three, but we hope to grow. As GeEK president, I do the fun, gross stuff, like poking things with a stick and collecting specimens. Sierra, our VP, is head researcher and Tierra is the treasurer/secretary. T does a good job, but it can be a challenge to read our club minutes written in glitter pen.

Today, good news travels in threes. I get to tell the twins that we are invited to Beaver Island, that I got Kenny, and maybe best of all, that the Buckthorns had left town for the entire summer. And because of the last bit of news, today I could pass through their yard unscathed.

The Hills' house is an explosion of color. I like it. It looks like a taco barn. Their turquoise and yellow house was surrounded by white daisies and pink and purple petunias. I rang the doorbell, then knocked and pounded on their red door.

When the door opened, an even greater explosion of sound burst out. It was a blend of classical music, annoying barking, toddler wailing, vacuum cleaner droning and the screeching-squawk of Tierra's cockatiel. And as usual, the first to greet me was the annoying barker, Goober, their drooly dog.

"Hey T, Hey Sie," I yelled.

"Hey, Holly!" Sierra opened the screen door. Cats bolted in every direction. Goober danced about, sniffing and slobbering all over my new cargo shorts. "He missed you," Sie said, handing me a paper towel.

nose power x 10!

GOOBER'S
Nose

KNOWS!

"I see that," I said, wiping off slime. Reason number one why I like snakes—they do not drool.

"That's his way of saying, 'What's new?' He learns

everything about everything with his nose," said Sierra. "Have a seat."

The center of the living room was a smelly pyramid of wet towels and sandy laundry topped with sea shells, plastic floaties, and bags of souvenirs. There was not a seat to be had.

"Hi, Holly," said Tierra, carrying out a plastic box with tubes poking out every which way. "Look what my dad got me. Willy-Nilly Hills, my new hamster." She held him up to me. The tiny, brown fur ball had a chamber for every activity imaginable. At the

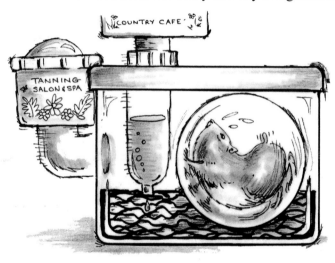

moment, the whirling Willy-Nilly was demonstrating his hamster gym wheel. I was so hypnotized by the furry, rolling beast I almost forgot why I came over.

"Guys, I have great news! Gram is taking us—all three of us, and my mom and Boy—to Beaver Island!"

"Sweet! Is that like Big Wolf Run Water Park or Goldilocks and Three Bears Golf and Slide Park?" asked Sierra, piling up towels. "When do we leave?"

"Um, actually I'm not really sure what it is," I said. I had left in such a hurry, I never asked Gram about Beaver Island. "But there will be lots of adventure," I continued. "We're leaving early tomorrow morning for a whole, entire week." Both of their heads snapped up.

"Holy cats! Tomorrow?" said Tierra. "We just got back."

"So you're packed then," I smiled. "Gram's meeting her sister there. It's Museum Week. They have music, an art show, a pet show and stuff."

"Art show!" Sie dropped the towels. "Cool! I want to enter."

"Pet show!" Tierra picked up the caged rodent. "I can enter Willy-Nilly. You hear that little fella? Your first show!"

"There *is* one small problem," I said and they both froze. "We need to go to your room for an emergency GeEK meeting."

We went in and sat on Tierra's glittery, cheery pink side of the room where a round, orange cat was napping.

"As my best friends and fellow GeEKS, I must warn you. My Aunt Kitty said that there's trouble on Beaver Island. I believe Team Wild has work to do there. This vacation could be a dangerous mission," I said.

"Holly," Sie said, "What's so dangerous about an island of beavers, unless a tree falls on someone?"

"Aunt Kitty needs our help," I said. "I can tell. It's a Wild thing. We should look up Beaver Island to see what we're dealing with." I knew Sie couldn't resist research, it's her specialty. So we moved over to her side of the room. Bookshelves lined the wall and her desk was covered with weather gauges, piles of golden National Geographic magazines, and notebooks. Pulling down a book on Michigan, she opened to the page on Islands of the Great Lakes.

"Beaver Island," Sierra read, "is the most remote island in Lake Michigan."

"That means we need plenty of supplies," I said. "What else ya got?"

"It says it's an unspoiled, unhurried island with museums, solitude, art galleries, shipwrecks and fishing. A large percentage of the island's population is Irish."

"I know," I said. "My relatives are from there. The islanders are practically family."

"Sounds nice to me," said Tierra.

"It wasn't always that way," continued Sierra. "The island, once used by Native Americans, trappers and traders, was later taken over by James Jesse Strang. He claimed the island as his own kingdom until angry mobs of fishermen did him in."

"Did him in?" gulped Tie.

"Aha! So there is trouble!" I said, jumping off the bed.

"But that was long ago, Holly," said Sierra.

"You know what they say, 'history repeats itself,'" I said. "Maybe trouble is coming back to haunt them. This could be dangerous."

"I just hope there aren't snakes. You know I hate snakes, Holly," squeaked T. I chewed on my thumbnail. Oops, I'd forgotten about that. My announcement about Kenny would have to wait.

"You guys, don't be silly. Museums, pet show, art show. What could possibly go wrong?" said Sierra, slamming the book shut.

"You never know. Ghosts, revenge, storms at sea," I said.

"It's a Great Lake, Holly," said Sierra.

"Big lakes get big storms. I'm just saying we need to be prepared, be on guard—and be ready at five a.m. sharp," I said as we walked to the front door.

"Storms. Hmm, I'll check for those," said Sierra. "Remember, Holly, we're going there to have fun."

"I know. Still, we need to be watchful," I called over my shoulder as I crossed the yard. I turned back just in time to miss stepping in a monstrous pile of Goober poo, only to trip and fall over his squealing rubber bunny toy.

"I hope you're more watchful than that!" laughed Sierra.

Dogs! I thought. I hoped there weren't any on the island. Holy creeps, it's always an adventure going to their house. Oh well, where we're going there'd be no Goober and way more adventure.

Right now, I had to pack for my very first northern expedition into troubled beaver country.

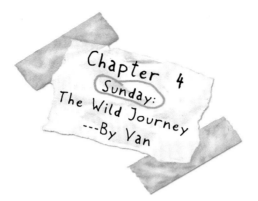

Chapter 4
Sunday:
The Wild Journey
---By Van

All night I kept thinking about how I, Holly H. Wild, would soon join the ranks of the Wild women. Pauline Bunyan, my axe-swinging, flapjack-flipping cousin from the Upper Peninsula, and Jenny Appleseed Wild, my great aunt who traveled the Northwest Territory, were both seasoned explorers by the time they turned twelve. Even my own grandmother, Gypsy Rose Wild, did some wandering of her own and once tackled a wild turkey outside Toledo. Of course, Daisy had them all beat when she wrassled a bear at only eight. Yep, I had some big shoes—or hiking boots, as the case may be—to fill. I was ready to break in my new, old daypack and cram it full of Wild adventure.

The girls showed up at five a.m. sharp wearing and carrying backpacks, swim fins, snorkels, and inflatable tubes. They looked like sleepy aliens hauling their mother ship of luggage behind them.

"What in the world did you pack?" I asked. "We're supposed to be roughing it!"

"The essentials," piped Sierra. "You said come prepared. I've got my camera, laptop, books, sunscreen, bug spray, rain ponchos, and umbrellas."

"Shampoo, conditioner, soothing salves, creams for burns, lotions for moisturizing, electric toothbrush, toothpaste, floss, art

Tie and Sie's Mothership!

supplies, hair ties, and clothes for a week," said T. "Oh, and Willy-Nilly's clothes for the pet show." The old boy was already up and churning on his wheel.

Boy slithered into the rear seat like black ink, and I handed Mom my daypack. I climbed into the van holding my "luggage"—I had stuffed three pairs of underwear and socks into my pillowcase.

"Holly, what all did you pack? It must weigh fifty pounds," she grunted, hoisting the daypack into the back.

"The essentials: specimen bottles, collecting bags, survival pack, portable pop-bottle-fishing kit, binoculars, my dead-thing-poking-stick, notebooks, a plastic spork and knife set, two pencils, a pen, flashlight, a spare pencil, my Great Lakes fossil collection, a string and ruler for tracking, granola bars, my lucky wildcat tail and stuff. And bear bells," I added.

"You won't need bear bells on the island. No bears there," chuckled Gram.

HOLLY WILD EXPLORER PAK contents

Great Lake fossils

explorer food

ACE PAINTS

poking stick

paper and pencils

portable pop bottle fishing kit
* hooks
* line (wrap line around bottle and rubber band it)
* cork bobber
* pill bottle (hold bobber and flies/lures)

"I came prepared. Anyway I like the sound they make," I said, sighing with relief. I had a real fear of bears. It's a Wild thing. The Wild women were notorious for their run-ins with ornery bears.

After everything was crammed in, Gram backed the sagging, creaking van down the driveway. At the end of the block, Mom gave us her 'When-you-wake-up-we'll-be-there' speech, her signal to settle down and go to sleep. I carefully fluffed up my pillow.

Sierra whispered, "The Beaver Island weather this week will be hot and humid with a chance of storms Thursday." I wasn't too worried. As an explorer kid I had a plan for dealing with weather—I simply ignored it.

By the time we got onto the highway, all was quiet—except for a snoring Boy and the occasional crunch of a snacking Willy-Nilly.

Just then an odor appeared that hung in the air like a foul blanket.

Heads went up. Windows went down. The girls checked their shoes. Gram checked gauges on the dash. Mom sniffed the box of cheesy crackers.

"What's that stench?" I asked. It was a cross between jalapeno three cheese corn chips, school cafeteria fish sticks, and two day old road kill.

Then Boy propped his huge rabbit feet over the back seat. We gasped and gagged. Mom made me cover them with a beach towel. Gram opened the vents and tuned the fan on high.

"Count the orange and white construction barrels, kids," Mom said, plugging her nose. "We'll be dere when you wake ub."

So everyone fell asleep—out of self-defense. Everyone except Gram and the ever-whirling Willy-Nilly.

Chapter 5
...And By Boat

The stench of Boy's feet worked like a charm. It had forced us to sleep *and* got us out of the van faster once we arrived. That was a good thing, because we woke to a blasting horn at the docks of the Beaver Island Boat Ferry Company. But it wasn't the boat, it was Gram honking.

Gram had dropped Mom off at the ticket office and parked the van next to a dumpster under a sign that read: *"Absolutely NO Parking! Violators Will Be Towed."*

"Let's go, troops," Gram said, dumping the van's contents in a heap on the curb. Half awake, we grabbed our gear and stumbled to the dock where Mom was waiting with our tickets.

"Wow! That boat's bigger than Ivy Buckthorn's house," I said as we filed through roped gates. Water slapped at the sides of the huge, white boat. On the side was a shamrock and *Emerald Isle* painted in green.

"On to Beaver Island, kids!" said Gram. "We'll be there in two hours. Ah, nature and clean, lake air. No fast food or malls." Sie and T suddenly snapped to attention and looked at me. Gram's announcement seemed to cause panic in the Team.

"No fast food? What do we eat?" asked Tierra, her eyes the size of two Junior Whoppers—with extra pickles. For a glittery princess, the girl's appetite could put Pauline Bunyan to shame.

"No malls? I thought this was going to be fun. I thought it was modern, not primitive," said Sierra, scowling at me.

"Oh it is, they just finished paving a road there," said Gram proudly.

"That sounds like wilderness," gulped Tierra. "Wilderness means snakes. You know I hate snakes." The twins looked like they were about to walk a gangplank.

We clanged up metal steps to the top deck where Mom did a head count. She turned for one last look on shore. "Whew! No bags left on the curb," she said, smiling. People down below waved. I waved back.

"This is so cool. From up here I can see our van," I said, waving at the people standing next to it.

Mom turned to look and her jaw dropped. She turned back to Gram and cried, "Mother Wild!" She must've noticed the van parked under that "Absolutely No Parking" sign.

"Relax. A nice man said I could park there. No one will notice." Mom looked back at the van and made a little whimpering sound. There it sat, rusted and red with "*WAsH Me 4 cRying Out lode*" on the rear window, bad spelling etched in thick Hayfields dust.

The boat revved its engines. Mom looked sick. She and the twins looked back at the town. All three looked like they wanted to jump ship.

The *Emerald Isle* blasted its horn. Gulls squealing like rusty hinges circled overhead. Mom and Gram dropped our mountain of gear onto the seats. Boy slithered onto a bench and plugged back in to his music.

Holly's OBSERVATION Game

Having a good memory is key to being a good naturalist. How many items can you remember after studying this luggage pile for 60 seconds? How many shoes? Toys? Drinks? Snacks? Bags?

MOM MONEY

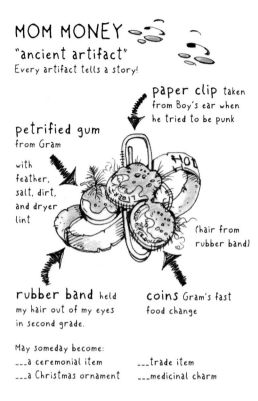

"ancient artifact"
Every artifact tells a story!

paper clip taken from Boy's ear when he tried to be punk

petrified gum from Gram

with feather, salt, dirt, and dryer lint

(hair from rubber band)

rubber band held my hair out of my eyes in second grade.

coins Gram's fast food change

May someday become:
___a ceremonial item   ___trade item
___a Christmas ornament   ___medicinal charm

"I'm hungry," said T, grabbing her rumbling stomach. I looked around.

"Vending machines!" I said. "Chippy-Chunky-Chewy bars sound good."

"Here," Mom said, fishing out change from her purse. Mom money— a handful of fuzzy quarters and dimes coated in spearmint gum and glued to a hairy rubber band and an old, rusty paper clip. Grub would cheer up the Team, especially chocolatey, chewy goodness. Mom joined Gram and some other women who were whipping out their cell phones showing off pictures of their kids and grandkids.

"Two hours," moaned Sie. There were no barrels to count out here, only floating, dead fish. I pulled out cards. Forty-two games of Go Fish!, twenty hands of rummy, six Chippy-Chunky-Chewy bars, and one nap later, the boat's horn blasted long and loud.

"There she is," Gram chimed. "The one and only Beaver Island. Still unspoiled and unhurried."

Sie and T sat up, their hair sticking out in every direction.

"I thought it would be more

wild looking," I said, rubbing my eyes. "Like beavers begging alongside the boat for sticks or something."

The boat's horn blasted again. More gulls squealed and circled lower and lower.

"Don't look up," Boy said, stretching.

The engines roared down to a grumbling drone. The boat backed into the dock. People gathered packages. Sailors in white hurried about with ropes.

Right then my stomach started doing funny floppy-turny things. I didn't know if it was excitement, worry about Tierra's snake fears, or the Chippy-Chunky-Chewy bars. But it grumbled and growled like the boat engines.

People waved from the docks below. The island's town was not so primitive after all. There were shops and houses and a handful of cars. It looked like any other small town and that made the twins happier. Things were looking up.

Maybe Sierra was right. What could possibly go wrong on an unhurried, unspoiled island out in the middle of one of the largest bodies of freshwater in the world?

Below us was a carnival of cats and dogs of every size and color wearing fancy scarves, bedazzled hats and jeweled leashes.

A girl carried a red parrot that mimicked the crowd's laughter. A guy with a green lizard on his shoulder had a matching dyed Mohawk. There was even a little kid dressed up as a turtle.

Gram and Mom scanned the crowd for Aunt Kitty. Boy bopped to a beat and kept an eye out for new friends.

"This is exciting," said Tierra, holding up Willy-Nilly's cage for him to see.

"Just remember, Team, we're here on a mission," I said. Something pale in the crowd below caught my eye. I blinked and looked again. I couldn't believe it.

Standing out like a rotting, steaming compost pile was mean, scowling Ivy Buckthorn. Just the sight of "Poison Ivy" makes me itch all over.

Mrs. Buckthorn and Ivy wore identical hot pink skorts that also matched the sparkly tutu and fairy wings their poodle, Queenie, wore.

The Buckthorn family is hard to miss, like a tacky highway billboard. Both Mr. and Mrs. B. had shocks of spiky, silvery-white hair. They were too tan, too loud and wore too much gold jewelry and fake smiles. They looked like sausages in gaudy clothing. When Mr. B. wasn't talking he was chewing on green onions. He isn't called "smelly old Buckthorn" for nothing.

Mr. B., looking like a rodeo clown in a blue paisley blazer, khaki shorts and sandals—with black dress socks—was chatting with a woman in a wheelchair. She was Gram's age with gray-streaked auburn hair. Dressed in turquoise and silver jewelry,

she seemed queenly and not the least bit amused with Mr. B's wild gesturing.

She impatiently tapped her ringed-fingers on the chair arms. A kid about Boy's age stood next to her chair, his messy, strawberry-blond hair hanging into his eyes.

Without warning, the woman in the wheelchair zipped off through the crowd like greased lightning. Holy creeps, could she move! The boy had to run after her. People jumped out of her way as she rocketed down the street.

"Hey, isn't that—?" T whispered to me.

"Ivy Buckthorn," growled Sie through gritted teeth. Sie dislikes Ivy more than I do.

"Oh, uh, I forgot to tell you guys," I stammered, "the Buckthorns are going to be out of town all summer. Looks like this is where they went."

"Oh, goodie," Sie sneered.

Then she saw us. Ivy's eyes locked onto us much like Kenny's eyes do when he spies his rat dinner. Sie and T looked ill again as we started filing off the crowded boat.

"Boy, it's hot," I said, feeling a little ill myself. I felt sticky and itchy. I had to get rid of my Chippy-Chunky-Chewy bar—now. I spotted a garbage can down below and tossed the melting candy bar towards it.

Sometimes, you just know you shouldn't do something, but you do it anyway, then after you do it, you really wish you hadn't. Well, this was one of those times.

As the candy bar made a graceful arc in the clear blue Lake Michigan sky, ten thousand gulls raced for it. When the winning gull snatched the bar midair, they all flew off in a screeching, squalling cloud leaving Ivy standing there, eyes wild, decorated from front to back with white streams of gull poop. Oops.

Right then, I tried to shrink and hide, as I chewed on my thumbnail.

Right then, Ivy's glare told me that if there was trouble on Beaver Island before, there was even worse trouble now, times ten.

Right then, I could hear the far off rumble of a storm and the yodeling of loons as Ivy turned beet red.

"I told you guys not to look up," snickered Boy. The teen guru in black had spoken.

Chapter 7
Wild Troubles

It turned out that it wasn't thunder or loons I heard. It was Ivy, who wailed like a tornado siren on a stormy night. People looked around like they should run for cover. Cats yowled, dogs cowered, and straggler gulls flew off from her shrill and sudden outburst.

A poo-painted Queenie yapped as Mrs. B. dragged Ivy and the dog through the crowd. Ivy turned for one last look at us, her long, blond ponytail cracking like a whip.

"That went well," snickered Sierra.

We got off the boat as the sailors unloaded the last of the cars with kayaks and canoes. Finally, a refrigerated semi-truck and tractor were unloaded.

T sighed with relief at the sight of the refrigerated truck. "They *do* have real food here," she said. I was relieved, too. I hadn't been so sure myself.

The tidal wave of pets and owners disappeared into town. In the distance, dogs barked and gulls squealed. The street was empty except for a small, redheaded woman in a large hat and dark sunglasses standing next to the pier, grinning.

"This is your Aunt Kitty," Gram beamed, hugging the tiny, lawn gnome of a woman in hiking boots and cargo shorts. Kitty Wild was nothing like I had imagined.

We faced each other. She was as tall as I was and had the same mop of Wild red hair poking out from her tan hat. But it was her vest that caught my eye. Each pocket had a pin of some kind—birds, animals or flowers. She tinkled as she moved. I liked her right away.

"Why, Holly, it's like looking in a mirror," giggled Aunt Kitty.

"Kitty's been all over the world, Holly. I knew you'd like to meet her since you're both Wild explorers," said Gram.

"It's really quiet here," T said, looking around. "Where are all the cars?"

"There aren't many. People use bikes or walk to get around," said Aunt Kitty. "I brought my car over to bring my equipment." She pointed to the forest green Subaru wagon.

The car had a bike and red kayak strapped on top with stickers covering the back windows. Out an open window poked the head of a brown and white basset hound. His ears and jowls nearly reached the ground. Great—a large, drooling D-O-G, dog!

"That's Hunter," Aunt Kitty said,

"He's my constant companion and goes everywhere with me. I only have room for one or two of you, but Huntie and I can drive your luggage to the hotel."

"Ride," said Gram, hopping in the front.

"Walk," Mom and I said as the dog sniffed the air. I clutched my pillow to my chest.

"Are you entering Hunter in the pet show?" Tierra asked Aunt Kitty.

"Huntie?" Aunt Kitty tittered. "Oh no, he'd snack on everything entered before they even got to the judging."

Tierra hugged her hamster cage tighter. "Willy-Nilly and I will walk, too, thanks."

Aunt Kitty loaded our gear into the trunk and rear seat, then Boy climbed in and draped his rag doll body over everything. Hunter sat in front with Gram and gnawed away happily on the tattered seat belt.

"We can talk more at lunch," said Aunty Kitty, slamming the hatch shut. "I have lemonade and sandwiches at the hotel.

As we walked through the town of St. James, the smell of food from the pub filled the air and made us drool like Hunter. Once at the hotel we all collapsed in the shade of a maple tree for lunch. Hunter chewed on a bone the size of a T-Rex leg as Aunt Kitty served us lemonade.

"Aunt Kitty, I thought Beaver Island was supposed to be unspoiled and unhurried. But it looks crowded and busy to me," I said, poking at purple flower sprigs floating in the pulpy lemonade.

"Those are lavender flowers, Holly. Puts a zip and some zing into lemonade," Aunt Kitty said. "Yes, Museum Week fills the island with tourists. After that, it gets quiet here again." Then she suddenly looked sad.

"Oh, I don't mind the flowers," I said, afraid I had hurt her feelings. "I only swallowed one. I learned to catch the others in my teeth."

"Oh no, Holly, it's not you. I'm sad because, as I wrote your grandmother, change is coming to the island. All these years, Beaver Island has been like a living museum. After this Museum Week, the island will never be the same again."

"But if the island is a living museum and museums preserve and protect valuable things like art, science, culture and history, how can that happen?" asked Gram.

MUSEUMS protect and preserve

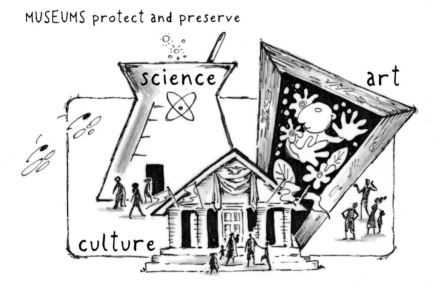

science

art

culture

"There's talk of building in the name of 'progress,'" sighed Aunt Kitty. "Islanders are unhappy and families and friends are feuding. Cinnamon Raisin Potato salad anyone?" Aunt Kitty offered. "Miss Tierra?"

"No thanks," T gulped. She never turns down food, but Aunt Kitty's salad ingredients made me shiver, too.

"Is all the building from beavers?" I asked.

"No, beavers are nature's builders. They benefit wildlife by building habitat or homes. The builders I'm talking about want to rip *out* habitat to make big money. They want to destroy wetlands to build a huge, indoor water park."

Builder
Beaver

"Some builders do a fine job," Gram said. "But it's a shame that others don't. Money is all some of them care about. When those builders leave, the plants, animals and people have to live with the changes."

"That's horrible! The animals won't have a place to go," Mom said. "They can't just hop on a boat to find a new unspoiled, unhurried island home."

"I knew this was a job for Team Wild," I said, nudging Sierra.

"What can we do, Holly?" asked Sierra. "We're just kids."

"Precisely," I said, popping a spoonful of Aunt Kitty's salad into my mouth—in the name of science and politeness. A strange feeling came over me. Not from the salad, but a feeling that somehow Ivy Buckthorn's family meant trouble for this unhurried, unspoiled island.

Something smelled fishy in this fishing town. And this time it wasn't Boy's feet.

Chapter 8
Snakes Alive!

After lunch we went up to our cozy apartment-like hotel room. Girls in one room, Gram and Mom in the other, and Boy on the living room couch.

The girls unpacked their things into empty drawers. They had it down to a system. Books, bottles, jars, socks, and t-shirts rolled tighter than Mom's ham and cheese roll-ups—everything had a place. Me, I heaved my backpack into the corner of the room and set my pillow carefully by the window in the sun.

"I'm unpacked. Let's explore!" I said.

"In a minute. Lunchtime for Willy-Nilly." Tierra pulled out his glittery travel bag and a can of green crunchy bits. "This'll make your coat glow for the pet show." Grabbing it from her hand, he popped it into his cheek pouch, and hopped back onto his treadmill to work it off.

T pulled out Willy's freshly ironed Western Rodeo Barbie hand-me-downs, a red flannel shirt and Levis on a pink hanger. "You keep eating like that and you won't fit into your chaps, mister," she cooed.

Sierra opened her computer bag and found a place to plug in her laptop. "Your aunt's cool. She looks just like you—only sparklier."

"Yeah, I'm glad we got to meet her. It's going to be fun here, but remember, we have a job to do," I said.

"Holly, I know you want to help, and your family came from here and all. But what can we do?" asked Sie turning on an old fan. "Whew, no air conditioner?"

"It'll come to me, guys. Meanwhile, we need to keep an eye out for Ivy. When she's around, there's trouble." I opened the window facing out into the woods. "This is awesome. I can't wait to study the island and find artifacts."

"I don't mind that it's primitive here," Tierra said, plopping down in front of the fan. "I just better not see snakes." I squirmed thinking about Aunt Kitty's snake lecture.

"Girls, there's a path down to the beach behind the hotel," Gram said, peeking her head in the door. She had on a Tigers baseball cap, bathing suit and a blue inner tube around her waist. "Don't forget we're meeting Kitty for dinner tonight in town."

"We might not have air-conditioning here, but there's a big, cold lake," Sie said, pulling out her swimsuit.

While the twins changed I went out on the balcony. The *Emerald Isle* blasted its horn as it left St. James Bay. We were on an island—totally surrounded by water. No way on and no way off. I looked down below. I could've sworn I saw Ivy under the tree where we had eaten lunch. Maybe Aunt Kitty's salad was causing me to have hallucinations because there wasn't anyone there now.

Tierra came out in a tangerine-striped suit with matching starfish hair bobs. Sierra was sporting her suit and cowboy boots and carried

Hold this picture of the Team 5 inches away from your face to see what fabulous creature they become! Creepy, times two!

a snorkel, fins, tube, and towel. "OK, let's go," she said. "We're ready for fun."

I grabbed my mini-exploring kit and shoved it into my pocket. Swimming was not my thing today. I felt more like tracking and collecting.

On our way to the beach the woman in the wheelchair zipped from the hotel towards town.

"She rolls faster than Willy-Nilly," I said, suddenly feeling itchy and looking around for Ivy. When we got to the beach I sighed with relief. No Ivy here. Tierra hopped onto her tube.

"I'm going exploring," I said.

"Suit yourself," Sie said, pulling off her boots.

I wandered up the beach in explorer-treasure-searching mode and collected tiny shells and feathers. Along the sandy path I sniffed

terns

cedar knees

dune grass

feathers, shells and sand sculptures

BEACH STUFF

fossils, garbage and dead fish

my way over to bunches of blooming, pink-flowered snowballs. Orange-and-black monarch butterflies fluttered about the sweet star-shaped flowers.

"Mmm-milkweed. So this is where you lay your eggs." I looked for the tiny white eggs under the leaves but found a yellow-and-black-striped caterpillar about the size of my pinky finger instead.

"Poor guy, must be boring eating nothing but milkweed your whole life. Kinda like eating broccoli every day," I said as I drew him and his poop in my book.

I heard a dry rustling in the grasses and stopped. The biggest garter snake I'd ever seen slithered out of the grass and across the sand, leaving behind railroad-like tracks.

milkweed munching monarch

"frass"

(caterpillar poop)

"Cool tracks! Your track is like an artifact—I better sketch it. It'll come in handy. Aunt Kitty might need these for her snake lecture. Stay away from Tierra," I called to the snake as I finished my sketch.

SNAKE Tracks

I heard more rustling and thought it was another snake, but when I looked up I saw the boy with the messy red hair that we had seen on the dock earlier. He was wearing a raggedy, white t-shirt with snakes on it. He looked as surprised as I was, then quickly turned and hurried back to the hotel.

"Whatcha doin', Holly?" Sie called, running up the path in her cowboy boots. Her swim mask covered half her face and her towel flapped like a cape behind her.

"Nothing. Looking. Stuff," I said, hiding my sketchbook in my pocket.

Sie eyed me suspiciously, then shrugged. "Your mom's looking for you. We've got to get ready for dinner." She trotted back to Tierra while I studied the snake tracks in the sand. The wind had already blown the tiny grains, wiping them away. It was a good thing I'd drawn them. Here one minute, gone the next.

While I was looking at the tracks a shadow passed across them. Then I got shoved backwards into the sand.

"Well, if it isn't Smellberry Shortcake," said Ivy with her hands on her hips.

"You changed your clothes, I see," I said, standing up.

Ivy scowled and turned bright red. "What is it with you and poop anyway?" she hissed. "You and your freaky friends better stay out of my way while you're here. And as an FYI, I'm going to win the art show *and* the pet show. My dad's taking care of that for me."

"That's cheating," I scowled back.

"That's life." Crossing her arms and whipping her ponytail, she twirled around and marched off. Keep your friends close, but your enemies closer, Gram says. And on this small island that wouldn't be hard to do. I was bound to run into Ivy—often.

Holy creeps! I hadn't been on the island for a whole day and it was already getting crowded. Of all the islands and all the lakes in Michigan, why did the Buckthorns have to come here to this one?

Chapter 9
Unhappy Islanders

On our way to meet Aunt Kitty for dinner we passed the Beaver Island School where we saw people bustling about. "How exciting, kids! This is where the art show is going to be," Gram said.

The artists grumbled and grimaced as they carried in canvases, crates, and bins. Snake-Boy from the beach carried a huge, gaudy painting through the door as the woman in her chair burst out like a turquoise arrow.

"Excuse me," said Sie to a tall, thin woman in glasses. "I want to enter my photography in the art show. Where do I sign up?"

"Inside," mumbled the woman over her shoulder. "Sorry, that was rude," she said, turning around. She shyly pushed up her glasses. "My name's Virginia Rail, reporter and photographer for the Beaver Island Beacon. Registration is just inside the school." She pointed and hurried off.

A short, gray-bearded man in a captain's cap and a huge man in a straw hat with long dark braids came out of the school. The big guy wore a t-shirt tie-dyed the colors of Superman ice cream under bib overalls. He carried a folding chair and a cardboard sign with pink and green balloons taped to it. It read: "ART SHOW: Monday thru Friday. Judging and prizes on Friday, 3 p.m."

"I need to get a shot of island life for my art show entry," said Sierra. "But everyone seems grumpy."

"Well, little lady, that's because of her, Old Sally," the bearded guy said, gesturing toward the bossy woman in the wheelchair.

"Vat is everyone shtanding around for? Moof! Moof people. Ve have a show to put on!" the woman barked, zipping past us.

"That's Sally Sonnschein. She was an island resident until she got a taste of fast and fancy New York life. Now, she's big time "Artist-on-the-Go." She's only been back here a few times since then, but returned yesterday to sell us out to a theme-park builder." The old man grunted and shuffled back inside.

"It's sad but true," the big guy said, wiping his brow. "Folks feel betrayed. We love our unspoiled, unhurried life. The theme-park will change Beaver Island. I'm Charlie Bird, and that's Rusty Wheeler," he said softly, shaking our hands. He was one huge guy, with one huge smile.

"We're island artists," Charlie said. "I'm a woodcarver and

Rusty's a painter. We're pleased to have you here for Museum Week. Tomorrow night there's Music on The Porch and I'll be telling stories afterward—with a campfire and marshmallows," he said winking.

"Mr. Bird, are stories artifacts?" I asked. "I'm an explorer collecting artifacts and information on Beaver Island."

"In a way they are. Stories are valuable and preserve a way of life. As a kid, my grandpa taught me that stories are even more important than food."

"Gosh," Tierra said, grabbing her growling gut again, "that *is* important. They should be in museums."

"If they were, then they'd be like those dusty, old stuffed birds and animals you see. No, stories need to breathe," Charlie chuckled. "I'd rather bring them out and share them."

"Awesome," I said and looked to Gram. "Can we go?"

Gram nodded, grinning, "Thanks, Charlie, we'll be there. Wouldn't miss a marshmallow toasting for the world."

When we got to the pub, Aunt Kitty was flitting about the patio handing out flyers to people at their tables.

"Please join us for our nature walks this week. I'm giving talks on the flowers and snakes of Beaver Island. Luckily for me, there are more snakes here than most any other island in Lake Michigan," she said, her eyes and smile twinkling.

Holy creeps! The snake was out of the bag. Tierra froze in her tracks. I really wished Aunt Kitty hadn't said that.

"S-snakes?" Tierra choked like a gasping trout.

"Good, you're all here," Aunt Kitty trotted up to us. "I took the liberty of requesting an outdoor table. Dining outside is such fun."

Tierra was as pale as the sand on the beach where I'd found the tracks only an hour ago. She didn't look very excited about dining outside, especially if snakes were dining outside, too.

"I've got a snake," I suddenly blurted out. The twins whipped around and stared at me open-mouthed. "His name is Kenny. He's a yellowy-orange corn snake." I don't know why, but it all came tumbling out my mouth. I guess since Aunt Kitty let the snake out of the bag, I'd bring mine out, too.

"You never told us you got a snake," said Sierra as we sat at the table.

"You were in Florida. I kinda forgot to tell you," I said shrugging.

"Too bad snakes here aren't that colorful. They'd be much easier to spot," said Aunt Kitty. "Michigan snakes are good at hiding and blending into their surroundings."

Holy creeps, times two! Aunt Kitty did it again. Tierra pulled her feet up into her chair.

"Don't worry Tierra, snakes are shy," Aunt Kitty said. "They won't bother you, and certainly can't eat you. Except for anacondas, which aren't found here—yet," she giggled. Geez, Aunt Kitty!

How could she be so cute and so creepy all at the same time?

"What about beavers?" I asked, changing the subject to something furry.

"Beavers are good at hiding, too. They're nocturnal creatures, active mainly at night."

The pub got busy and waiters rushed about the patio. Then through the crowd rolled Sally Sonnschein and Snake-Boy in his raggedy shirt. She wore royal purple and a silver necklace that had a sun and the letter 'S' on it. She waggled her ringed-fingers ordering the staff about.

"She acts like she's the queen of Beaver Island," I said.

"Sally's quite the VIP, she's the pet show and art show judge this year," said Aunt Kitty.

So that's how Ivy's going to win both shows. Her dad must've been at the dock bribing Sally to pick her crummy art and creepy dog to win first place.

Aunt Kitty handed us a flyer of the week's events:

BEAVER ISLAND MUSEUM WEEK EVENTS

Monday: Pet Show Registration, Wildflower Wander, Music on The Porch, Campfire Stories: Native American Legends and Lore.

Tuesday: (Print Shop/Museum Talks) Strang: King for a Day?, Stories of the Good Doctor Protar, Beaver Island Head Lighthouse Tours.

Wednesday: Snakes Alive! Lecture & Wild Wonders Walk, Beaver Island Artist's Party.

Thursday: Beaver Island Herp Hike and Picnic.

Friday: Art Show Judging with Cash Prizes and Awards, 3 p.m. at the School; Pet Show Parade and Judging on the Porch.

"What's a 'herp picnic'?" T asked. "Are herps served at the picnic? What do they taste like?"

"Oh no, we're not eating them! Herpetology is the study of amphibians and reptiles," explained Aunt Kitty. "The picnic is the island's celebration of those animals, who we call 'herps' for short."

"Uh, that's…interesting," T said.

Interesting? I jumped up from the table. Wow! This was going to be an awesome week!

"Tomorrow I'm going exploring!" I said.

"Tomorrow I need to get pictures," Sierra said.

"Tomorrow I need to register Willy-Nilly," Tierra said. "And iron his outfit. Maybe I'll add glitter to his hat. Anything to beat Queenie in her pink tutu."

I didn't have the heart to tell her what Ivy had told me.

Chapter 10
Monday:
Out of the Bag

When we got up Monday morning, Mom and Boy had already left for the beach. Mom's plans for the week were to be reading, relaxing, and resting. And Boy's plans were to be her skinny, black shadow because she was the one with the money.

Tierra went through her bug spray and sunscreen ritual as Sierra packed her fanny pack with her camera, a water bottle, and rain gear. I pulled my clothes and fossil collection out of my backpack to make it lighter and pulled down my exploring hat.

"Where are you girls heading today?" asked Gram. "Beach, library, or the Toy Store Museum?"

"Library," said Sierra, checking her camera batteries.

"Toy Store Museum!" said T, shouldering her life-like furry puppy purse. Its tongue, legs, and tail waggled wildly. I just couldn't seem to escape dogs, ever.

"I want to explore, but the toy store sounds like a museum I wanna see," I said, sliding on my pack.

"Visit each place, then go exploring," smiled Gram. "Breakfast is on the table. I'm heading out soon to Kitty's Wildflower Walk."

"So how's Willy-Nilly doing?" I asked T. "I haven't heard him running in awhile."

"He must be tired. Resting up for his trip to town today," said Tierra. She opened the tank and fed Willy an orange crunchy treat. "Wow, he does have an appetite." She tried stroking his brown chins but he jumped away. "Feeling nervous today, fella? I hope it's not stage fright." T shrugged and replaced the lid. She and Sie went to the kitchen.

Now was my chance.

I went over to my pillowcase—and pulled Kenny out.

It had been a long ride for him. "You look pretty pale, Ken. Probably from being cooped up." He played on the chair while I made the bed. When I looked back I spied him slithering past my feet. "Holy creeps, you're fast, mister," I said, picking him up. He curled around my arm. That's when Tierra walked in.

"I forgot my-y-y— YARRRGH!" she screamed. She jumped onto the bed and plastered herself to the wall. To say she freaked out would be putting it mildly. Kenny's head poked out from my sleeve. "Holly Wild! GET THAT OUT OF HERE!"

NAME THAT DANCE!

Phoney Balogna

The Freak

Funky Chicken

INVENT your own _____

Gram and Sierra ran in to see what happened. Kenny flicked his tongue and stared at us with pinkish eyes.

"Holly H. Wild, what in the world is Kenny doing here?" asked Gram, snickering.

"I brought him for the pet show. I didn't want to leave him home with Dad, so I was keeping him in my pillowcase like the Reptile Hunter does on TV," I said, chewing on my thumbnail.

"Pillow case!" Sierra and Tierra said.

"Sweetie, he needs a proper place to stay. He can't live in your pillowcase all week," Gram said, scratching her head. "Wait here. I'll find something."

"Does he bite?" asked Sierra, sitting on the edge of the bed. Kenny flicked his red tongue.

"Nope," I said tickling his tail.

Tierra peeked through her fingers. "Don't let him go."

"I won't. I was keeping him a secret so you wouldn't freak out. Anyway he won't hurt you. It's not like you're a mouse. That's what he eats."

"HOLLY! Don't say that!" screeched Tierra, her eyes as big as melons. "What about Willy? What if he eats Willy? Willy-Nilly is like a mouse."

"He won't eat Willy. Kenny is here and Willy-Nilly is there." I pointed.

Sierra went over to Willy-Nilly's cage. "He's fine." The tank lid was slightly ajar. She spun the silent wheel and dug through the green colored shavings.

"Holly," she said, pushing up her glasses, "we have a problem."

I gulped hard and looked over at Tierra. She looked like a kettle about to boil over.

"WILLY!" Tierra bellowed. She ran to his cage. "Where's Willy-Nilly?" She opened up the circular outdoor critter café section of his hamster habitat. They both looked at me like I had eaten the whirling, furry beast myself.

"I don't know." I shrugged. They looked at Kenny. And then I looked at Kenny. Right into his pearly-pink eyes. He smiled his snakey smile.

"Holly Wild!" wailed Tierra, scrunching up her body into a tight coil. Her purple-red face made her green hair glitter stand out.

"Guys. No way. He couldn't have gotten Willy. I'm sure of it."

Tierra collapsed onto the bed in tears. "I fed him this morning. His last supper. How could you Holly? You're my best friend. Willy-Nilly was a gift. I was going to win first place!"

"I-I'm sure Willy is OK," I reassured her. "Are you sure you closed his cage?" T and Sie both shot me a look. "Just asking," I shrugged. The twins had that blending-into-one-angry-best-friend thing going again.

"That doesn't matter now, Holly," said Sierra. "He couldn't just disappear." The girls were franticly searching the room when Gram came in with a large pickle jar.

"Success! From the storage room in the basement," Gram said, holding up the jar. "The woman at the desk let me borrow it until Kitty can get—Oh dear, what now?" Gram froze.

"Willy-Nilly's gone. He did it," both girls pointed at Kenny.

"No, he didn't. I never let him out of my sight," I squeaked.

Gram punched holes in the lid and slid Kenny inside. I put in some fossils for him to crawl on, and placed a clean t-shirt in with him so he could hide. Which is a good thing, because the look on T's face was not particularly friendly.

"You girls go ahead," said Gram. "I'll keep looking for Willy-Nilly. He'll show up. Let's leave his cage open with some food. He's a hungry little devil, that one. Don't worry. You can still register him in town for the pet show."

It was a long, quiet walk into town. "Why don't we go to the toy store first? They have the best candy around," I said, hoping to cheer Tierra. Sierra found the store on the Beaver Island map.

"What if Kenny ate him? What if I never see his fat little belly ever again?" snuffled Tierra.

"Don't worry," said Sierra. "Wait and see. There's the Print Shop. Let's run in and register Willy and Kenny." We finished our paperwork and looked around at the shop's books and maps before heading out.

The day was getting hotter. After walking for what seemed like forever, we came to what looked like a weedy, overgrown yard. "This is where the toy store should be," said Sie looking around. "But where is it?"

I stood on my toes. There, behind all the flowers, I could see a weathered gray building. We found a narrow path and followed it through the tall weeds. The wild garden smelled so good that it drew us in like the butterflies that danced over the flowers. It was like an enchanted world from a storybook.

Old metal toys, trucks, and cement statues were hidden everywhere. It was as if little kids went inside and left their toys laying around—a hundred years ago.

"Your Aunt Kitty would like this. There are flowers of every kind and color," Tierra said, peering through wildflowers taller than me. "You almost need a machete in this jungle," she laughed.

Recycled Garden Art

GATHER: buttons, keys, old game pieces, dice, toys or shells and stones you find outside. PRESS items into air-drying clay and let dry. Place your garden art among plants in your room to make it cheery.

We went inside. Wow! Bins of candy, chests of tiny dolls, shelves of rocks, books, and art supplies filled the room from floor to ceiling. Each aisle was packed with the wonderful goodness of treats and toys. This was my kind of museum! The screen door slammed nonstop as kids came in and crowded the store.

"This museum is awesome times ten! Look—fossils for my collection!" I picked out a handful of ancient and rare stone treasures.

"This place is like something out of Harry Potter!" said T, gazing up at toys suspended over her. "It's magical."

"Sweet!" announced Sie, "*A Sky and Weather Quick Flip Book.*"

Right then Tierra squealed, "*Michigan Tales Book 4: Wild and Wooly Tails of The Good, The Bad, The Ugly.*" I've been waiting for this since I got *Book 3* last year." She picked it up and flipped through the pages. "This copy was signed by the author!" She set it down to get out her wallet as her pooch purse waggled in approval.

Just then the door slammed extra loudly and I started to itch. I turned to look and saw Ivy Buckthorn come stomping in, her blond ponytail swinging, clearing the aisle.

"Well, if it isn't Strawberry Shortstuff and her pathetic pals. I didn't think you guys could afford toys, let alone a trip to Beaver Island," she said to Sierra. My freckles sizzled and Tierra and I grabbed Sie's arms.

"Why don't you go play with the sea gulls?" Sierra suggested.

"I can't because I'm busy spending lots of money—on art supplies. I don't even really need to since my dad is making sure I will win," Ivy said with a smirk. Her eyes locked on the book that Tierra had just laid down. Then Ivy snatched it up.

Tierra gasped. Her pooch purse quivered, its tail ducking between its fake fur legs.

Ivy examined the cover. "Cool book." She played with the pages. Tierra whimpered.

"I didn't think you knew how to read," Sierra said.

Ivy glared at her and snapped the book shut. "It looks like I will be tonight." T looked devastated. Sie looked angry.

"I'll bet her picture's in there under 'Ugly,'" I whispered to Sie. Ivy must've heard because she whipped around. She shook all over like she was going to explode. Then she grabbed boxes of fudge with walnuts and packages of Wacky Crackle candy and stacked them on top of the book.

She was still shaking as she tried to push her way through the aisles when someone yelled, "Watch out!" Snake-Boy burst through

the door and bumped into Ivy. Hard.

Ivy was plunged into the candy bins, and her tower of treasures toppled. Her sparkly, silver sneakers were the last things I saw as she went head over heels to the floor. Rainbows of gumballs rolled. Green Gummy Frogs bounced. And Ivy squirmed in the mess on her belly, trying to get up. Sie and I were so busy laughing that we missed the rest of the excitement.

"Stop! Thief! That kid's a thief," someone yelled. "He just stole candy." The door slammed and Snake-Boy was gone. We looked back, and Ivy was gone, too. She had dropped everything and left unnoticed.

Tierra picked up the precious book and dusted it off. Sierra picked up the fudge that Ivy had stacked on top and bought the whole bunch. The store owner gave us sourballs to thank us for helping pick up the mess. When we got outside Tierra was laughing, too.

"Wow, did Ivy grab air or what?" Sierra chuckled. "I wish I'd gotten a picture of that. I'm glad that kid knocked her over. She deserved it."

"Yeah, he sure put Ivy in her place. Still, stealing's uncool," said Tierra. "Maybe he's poor. He does wear raggedy clothes."

"Maybe so, but I'd have given him money just to see Ivy flying through the air," Sierra said, giggling.

"Maybe he's a spy for Sally Sonnschein and Mr. Buckthorn. He is kinda her servant. And he was watching me on the beach yesterday," I said. The twins looked at me.

"Why didn't you say something, Holly? Maybe he took Willy-Nilly. I wouldn't put it past Ivy to send him after Willy-Nilly so she could win the pet show," T fumed.

"We need to be calm," Sie said. "All three of us need to keep our eyes open."

"Holy creeps, the list is growing. We have to be on the lookout for creepy Ivy, hidden snakes, a thieving spy, and approaching storms," I sighed.

Chapter 12
Snake Tails

For an unspoiled, unhurried island it was anything but boring.

Shopping always makes Tierra feel better. So by the time we got back to our hotel she had forgotten the morning's events and was happy again. Gram had moved Kenny to a new home, a roomy tank borrowed from the island's biological school.

"I don't understand why Willy-Nilly left. He had an awesome home, food, and water," T said, staring at his empty cage. "Maybe it was his cowboy outfit."

Home, food, and water. Tierra's words reminded me of the troubles Beaver Island's wildlife would face when the theme park was built.

Tierra fluffed the bedding in Willy's lookout lodge and dropped in another treat. The little guy was off on his own island adventure.

"He'll turn up," said Sierra. "Maybe you can make a paper doll of Willy-Nilly for the art show and dress it in his outfit."

Tierra nodded. "Yeah, that would be cool."

I looked in on Kenny in his new home. He had everything he needed, but he wasn't moving much. I tried to pick him up but he buzzed his tail. Gram says that sometimes they do that when they don't want to be disturbed, so I let him be. Maybe he has snake gas or something.

During the heat of the day we hung out and relaxed. Beach time, reading time, art time. It was good to kick back.

"Hey guys, let's get ice cream," I suggested. We grabbed our gear. Sie got her camera, T carried their sunscreen/bug spray kit, and I grabbed my mini-exploring kit. As we headed to town, we passed the artists trudging into the school with more things.

"I feel so bad for all of them, they seem so sad," Tierra said. "I don't feel like ice cream now."

"Me neither," sighed Sie.

Like the home of the island's wildlife, the artist's home would be changed by the theme park, too. "Team Wild," I said, pulling my hat down, my brain churning, "we've got to do something. But what?"

Tierra and Sierra shrugged and sighed. "Don't worry, Holly," Sie said, "We'll think of something."

Later we met my family at the beach for our picnic dinner, and we forgot about the sad artists for a while. As it got later, people began lining the beach to watch the sun set. I was relieved that Ivy was nowhere to be seen.

"I have to say you girls are real sports," said Gram. "No A/C in the hotel. No fast cars, no fast food on the island. No TV or video games. Just look at you!"

"It's been fun roughing it," said Tierra, grinning.

"It's cool," said Sierra. "It's like a challenge thinking of other ways to do things."

"Sunsets instead of TV, art instead of video games, picnics instead of fast food. I like it," I said.

We walked the beach looking for fossils and filled Gram's socks with our favorites. It was a beautiful evening and we watched for the "green flash" over the water that everyone talked about. "It happens when conditions are just right," said Mom. But not tonight, which

Take Holly's Beaver Island CHALLENGE!

Draw a line from something you usually do and replace it
with something new you might try.

picnics

video games

storytelling

reading

fast food

art and
writing

sunset and
nature watching

TV or computer

was OK—if it happened all the time it wouldn't be special. We sat
in silence while others applauded the sunset.

"Who'd think a sunset could be so magical," sighed Tierra,
relaxing in the grass. For a moment she'd forgotten all about her
snake fears.

As it got darker we headed to the Print Shop, where people had
gathered for the storytelling. Crickets chirped and fireflies bounced
in the grasses like tiny fireworks. Everyone oohed and ahhed at the
yellow banana moon hanging over Lake Michigan. The deep-blue
night sky was a stage curtain sprinkled with stars.

"You can see stars so clearly here," said Mom. Boy pointed out

the stars in the Summer Triangle and the Milky Way that stretched from one end of the island to the other.

"You see stars here you wouldn't see anywhere else," Gram said. "Another reason to keep the island from being spoiled. More lights make it harder to see the stars."

Soon the fire was roaring and out stepped Charlie Bird. He wasn't wearing his overalls and straw hat. He was in an embroidered vest, woven belt and wore a bird foot necklace. He placed a bundle of sweet-smelling herbs in the fire.

"Welcome," he said. "I'm Charlie Bird, an Odawa storyteller. To celebrate Museum Week, I will be telling very special Native American stories, ones handed down to me from my grandparents' grandparents," he said, grinning.

His stories are just like Gram's stories about Daisy and the other Wild women. They're my family's artifacts.

"Stories belong to everyone who listens with their ears and with their heart," Charlie began. The big guy moved like a ballerina as he told stories about animals changing color, and shape, and behavior. Each one began with "Long ago, when the earth was new and the animals and the trees could talk." It was better than TV.

The moon disappeared, the fire crackled, and the crowd hushed as Charlie started his last story. Even the crickets stopped their chirping.

"This final story is about a special hero," he said, picking up a white bow with a black feather tied to it and placing a beaded fur quiver of arrows over his shoulder. I recognized the fur—a wildcat. I touched the tail on my bag and wondered if Charlie was a Wild, too. He did have freckles.

"Long ago, when the earth was new and the animals and trees could talk, our hero, Manabozho, was out naming the plants and animals. He came to a large, beautiful lake, the same one you see behind you. A giant snake, the King of Serpents, lived there and had been coming out of the water killing all the animals. Manabozho

told the snake, *'Stop killing my friends!' But the snake refused."* Charlie sighed, then continued.

"So Manabozho did what he had to do. He hunted the snake with his bow. Each time the serpent crawled out of the water, Manabozho would shoot. And Manabozho would miss! 'If only I could get a closer shot at him, I can save my friends,' he thought. Then Manabozho had an idea. 'I am Manabozho, I can change my shape!' So he turned himself into a big

pine stump and put himself right by the water. When the snake came out, he looked around and saw the stump. 'I'll bet that ssstump is Manabozzzho trying to trick me,' he hissed."

"So the snake wrapped himself around the stump and squeezed. And he squeeeezed and squeeeeeeezed with all his might. 'It mussst be a ssstump!' Exhausted, the snake turned and slunk towards the water. So Manabozho turned back into his human form and drew his ash bow with the jasper-tipped oak arrow— and let it fly. The arrow flew true and hit its mark."

Just like the story, right then Charlie became Manabozho as he held the bow triumphantly. People gasped and others clapped.

"But," Charlie continued, *"it didn't kill the snake, it only wounded him. The snake slithered into the water hissing, 'Manabozho, I am going to kill you and all of your animal friendsss!' And with that, caused a great flood to come upon the earth."* The crowd groaned. A hero's troubles are never over.

"But Manabozho was quick!" Charlie clapped his hands. Surprised, everyone jumped and then laughed. *"He chopped down a great cedar tree and made a canoe for him and his friends to climb into. And they were all saved."*

"Thank you. Megwetch," said Charlie, bowing as people clapped wildly. Then they stood and stretched and picked up sleepy children.

"Mr. Bird, are those stories true?" I asked as he was gathering his things.

Charlie smiled and winked at me. "Sometimes stories…are not just stories."

By the dying firelight, I spied a black feather where we had been sitting and tucked it in my backpack. Right then a shooting star zipped across the sky, a bright streak over the dark lake.

"Manabozho's arrow," I whispered.

This was way better than TV.

Chapter 13
Tuesday:
Island Kings

"Maybe today," Tierra sighed, laying a hamster highway of neon-colored food leading to the empty cage.

"Ivy must be hiding out after the toy store incident yesterday. She wasn't at the fire last night," I said, eating my PBJ toast. I spent all night thinking about Manabozho's cleverness helping the animals and wondering what I could do to help the island. I guessed it would come to me when the time was right.

Gram and Mom were finishing up breakfast dishes when Aunt Kitty came to the door.

"Good news, good news," she chirped, "Fox Lake is prime habitat for beavers and snakes. I'm taking you kids out there today to help me gather information for my talk tomorrow."

"Sweet!" I said leaping up. "I want to see real live wild beavers and snakes!"

"Snakes? No thanks," Tierra said shivering. "Last night's story was enough for me. I can't sleep knowing Kenny's in the next room."

"Come on," Sie nudged Tierra. "Watching an empty cage won't bring Willy back."

We climbed into Aunt Kitty's green car, shoving piles of papers, clipboards holding papers, and books and boxes stuffed with papers aside. Every nook and cranny held something—a pen, a pebble, a dried flower—and lots and lots of dog hair.

Driving down King's Highway, the island's only paved road, people out walking and biking waved as we passed. Each time they did, we waved back. We were becoming Beaver Islanders.

On the way out of town, Aunt Kitty told us how the highway was named for King Strang and how he had declared himself king and strutted about town in a paper crown. I imagined Mr. Buckthorn as king, strutting around with his hair spiked into a crown. Gross.

"King of Beaver Island" James Jesse Strang

A large black-and-blue butterfly fluttered across the road in front of us. "Look girls, an eastern swallowtail!" Kitty exclaimed. "Female!"

"Aunt Kitty, how do you know so much about nature stuff?" I asked.

"It's quite easy, Holly," said Aunt Kitty. "Even though I went to college to become a biologist, I am also a naturalist. A naturalist can be anyone who is curious about nature and not afraid to ask questions or explore the world."

"Hey, that's me!" I said. It was good to know I was on the Wild path.

"One way for a naturalist to make sense of nature and what they see is by using the Scientific Method," she said.

"That sounds mysterious," I said.

"Asking questions about something you see is the first step," Aunt Kitty said. "That's called making an observation. Next, you answer your question with a guess. That's making a hypothesis. Collecting and organizing information and doing experiments help prove if your guess is correct."

"I'm good at collecting and experimenting," I said.

"And we're good at organizing," said Sierra.

"Lastly, you draw a conclusion, which answers your first

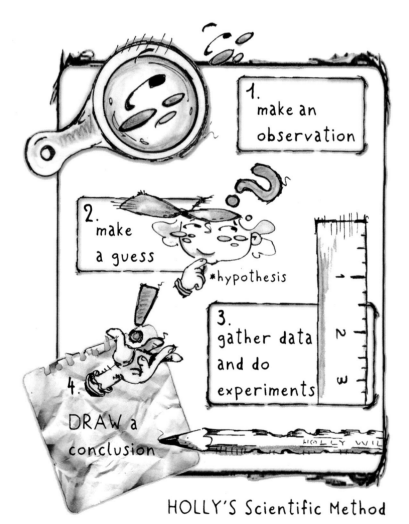

1. make an observation

2. make a guess
*hypothesis

3. gather data and do experiments

4. DRAW a conclusion

HOLLY'S Scientific Method

question. You present your findings and voila! You now know more about something. The Scientific Method can be an important tool."

"A tool that's easy to pack," Sierra joked.

"Ask questions, get the facts, think things through before I act. I get it." Now I had another scientific tool to use.

"Tell us about beavers," I said to Aunt Kitty.

"Well, beavers are North America's largest rodents," she said. "Like all rodents, their teeth constantly grow, so they have to chew. Like human builders, beavers change the landscape, but they use their teeth. Their tree cutting, dam building, and flooding creates new habitat. New habitat equals new food and homes for wildlife. Beavers are nature's engineers," said Aunt Kitty, as we pulled up at the lake.

"And beavers don't use smelly machinery," Tierra said, pointing to a yellow bulldozer by the road.

The NEW WORLD BEAVER
(Castor canadensis)

Busy as a beaver?
Beavers spend most of the day resting, grooming playing and eating.

Team work!

TRUE OR FALSE?

- People used to believe that beavers could carry mud on their TAILS.

- The beaver was once classified as a FISH.

TRUE to both statements. We now know that beavers use their leathery tail as a rudder and prop.

Even though beavers are excellent swimmers and their tails look scaly like a fish, they are warm-blooded mammals. They have fur and give birth to live young that they nurse.

Next to the bulldozer was a sweaty Mr. Buckthorn, hammering up a sign. He had a green onion stalk dangling from his mouth, and it reminded me of Kenny and the rat's tail. After he sped away we got out to look at the new sign.

Buckthorn Builders Inc., Future site of the Extra-Extravaganza Pool Park and Mini Mall. It *was* Buckthorn who brought unrest to the island! I knew he was up to no good.

On the sign was a castle with an indoor pool, water slide, and mini golf-course. Inside, big screen TVs were scattered throughout. There was virtual video badminton, virtual snow-shoeing, and a virtual toboggan run. Taco, burger, and pizza food court areas were on each end of a painted hiking trail edged with artificial trees and vinyl turf.

The heated indoor pool had a fake beach complete with non-pooping, stuffed gulls. It was "nature", neat and tidy, and all under one roof. No hot, no cold, no sun, no rain. Nothing was really real.

"This," said Aunt Kitty, "is what is happening to Beaver Island. Homes for flowers and wildlife will be destroyed for this. Parks are good for people and nature. But an indoor theme park on an unspoiled, unhurried island is unthinkable and most certainly unwanted."

"Unbelievable," said Sierra. "No wonder the people living here are so upset."

"He wants to keep out nature with a roof and walls," said Tierra. "Everything on this sign is unnatural and unhealthy."

"Mr. Buckthorn will be the new King Strang of Beaver Island," I said. "And this is his new colony."

Extra-Extravaganza
Pool Park & Mini Mall

coming soon!

NO fuss
e!

terslide
rts, video

Buckthorn Builders Inc.

"No man is an island," said Aunt Kitty, shaking her head.

Chapter 14
Treasures and
Tracks

"What'll happen to the beavers? Can they be moved to a new home?" I asked Aunt Kitty.

"They will likely be trapped and killed," Aunt Kitty said sadly. "Beavers can't be relocated. Their colonies are marked with scent to keep other beavers out. It works. New beavers moving into another's territory means big trouble for newcomers."

"Poor beavers," Tierra said. Then she jumped as she stepped on a stick. "Oh, I thought it was a snake."

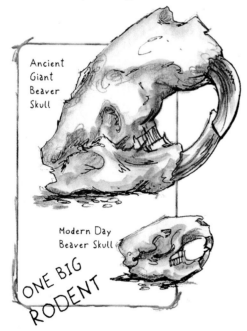

Ancient
Giant
Beaver
Skull

Modern Day
Beaver Skull

ONE BIG
RODENT

"Were there really giant snakes here long ago, Aunt Kitty?" I asked.

"Michigan has fossil evidence of long, snake-like creatures, sharks, and even walruses. Fossils of extinct giant beavers were found here. Back then, the beaver relatives were six to eight feet long, as large as our black bear."

"Awesome, times ten!"

I said. I imagined a beaver the size of Aunt Kitty's car swimming across the lake with Hunter riding on its back.

"Beavers aren't that big anymore," Aunt Kitty said. "Too bad they aren't. Finding something rare like that living on the island would save it." An idea formed in my brain as Aunt Kitty's cell phone rang with a loon yodel.

"It's the bio station. I have to take this call. I'll catch up with you kids later," she said, walking off.

Down by the lake, bees hummed, birds twittered, and a woodpecker tapped as my idea grew.

"This lake is so peaceful," said Sierra. "It washes everything away. It really cleans your hard drive."

"Wait until machines start roaring," T said, launching wood chips like tiny boats in the water.

"That's it, GeEKS! We need to find something unusual or rare to save the island!" I blurted. "We have to start looking!"

"Like what?" asked T.

"I don't know, artifacts or something. But this is as good a place as any. Let's follow the dragonflies."

Huge dragonflies darted and danced, flashing their wings in the hot sun. Some were blue and green, larger than my hand. T's book said that they used to be as big as hawks! Huge bullfrogs bellowed and fish lips smacked the undersides of lily pads. Everything seemed bigger here.

"Look, there's a trail over here," I called, tripping over

a tree root. "Holy creeps! Now I know why they call these cedar knees. If you're not careful, you might end up on your own knees."

We followed the narrow trail of deer tracks through the cedars when I nearly stepped on a fishing lure. The red spoon had rusty, wicked looking hooks.

"Yikes! I better pick that up before someone or something gets caught in it," I said, carefully wrapping it up to throw away later.

We kept going and I found another lure tangled in a tree by the shore. This one looked like a yellow frog wearing a skirt.

It had a wide, red mouth and big pop-eyes.

"It could be a valuable artifact. It does look real old and hand-painted," I said, putting it into my bag.

"People can be so thoughtless," said Sie. "What'll it look like when lots of people come here?"

Sierra found a mussel shell and empty turtle egg shells underneath some ferns. We put those in my collecting bag. Then I found two quarters and three dimes. This was turning into quite a good exploration!

The trail got more narrow, the cedars thicker and more tangled. The woods seemed darker. It was

TURTLE EGG SHELLS

Kinda look like crushed ping-pong balls.

so quiet, only a woodpecker's tap-tapping and the lake's lap-lapping made any sound.

Remembering the story from last night gave me chills. Suddenly a loud splash and a yodel came from the lake. We all jumped, then laughed.

"It's a loon," said Sie. "Of course, I forgot my camera back in the car." The girls crept to the shore for a better look, while I checked out tracks by the water's edge.

This was a regular animal highway. But these weren't deer tracks. Deer have two toes. Some of these had three toes, some had

CRITTER HIGHWAY!

Water brings all kinds of animals to the shore.

DRAW the track of the last animal who crossed the trail.

four and one had five. Too weird! None of these were tracks I'd ever seen before.

A rustle in the ferns got my heart pounding. What the heck was in there? And what the heck was that smell? Kinda barn-like, like Boy's socks.

"Hey guys," I whispered, "I think we're onto something." There was another rustle in the brush. The nattering woodpecker darted past me when out of the ferns charged a curious, shiny-eyed chipmunk.

"Rats!" I said, clutching my pounding chest.

"Nope, just another rodent relative of the beaver," laughed Sierra.

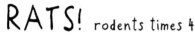

beaver   chipmunk   Willy-Nilly   Buckthorn

"Rodents and snakes. Holy creeps, this island is filled with them," I said.

"Don't remind me," said Tierra, turning back. But splashing sounds nearby caught my attention. Lily pads rippled and rocked from something moving below. Stepping closer, I spotted something lying on the shore.

On the muddy bank was a wrinkly, brown thing as long and thick as a human arm, covered with scaly bumps. Hello! Now here was a curious thing.

"Hey! I found something," I called, excitement creeping up my spine like a slithering snake.

"Another lure?" Sierra called.

Tierra ran down the trail then backed up. "Gross," she said, wrinkling her nose. "What is it?"

"I don't really know," I said. "It looks prehistoric, or like a hunk of a big snake. A REALLY big snake. It's at least four times thicker than Kenny, and he's four feet long!" Something I'm sure T did not want to hear.

"It looks more like some dead person's arm," said Sierra, leaning over it.

"Big snake or arm. Either way, let's go," Tierra urged.

"Who knows what could be living on an unhurried, unspoiled island in the middle of one of the biggest freshwater lakes in the world," I said. "Remember, Aunt Kitty did say there used to be weird, prehistoric animals around here."

GROSS!

"What if it's the tail of that giant snake in Charlie Bird's story? He did say that stories are not just stories," Tierra said, her eyes as big as pinecones. We all stared at the thing. This got me to thinking about Aunt Kitty's comment about the anaconda: *They're not here— yet.* A snake this size could do some serious squeezing, like the snake in Charlie's story.

"Team Wild," I said, "I think I've found evidence of some ancient, undiscovered snake."

"Holly, you're jumping to conclusions—form your hypothesis," reminded Sie.

"But I'm sure about this," I said, feeling squishy inside. "Well, pretty sure anyway."

"We'll get our tools and come back and study it. Then we'll draw our conclusion," Sie said. Just then I heard Aunt Kitty calling us. I turned to look at the very thing that could save the island. I really wanted to pick it up but I didn't have a plastic bag with me.

"Holly H. Wild, you're not bringing that disgusting thing back with us," warned T, reading my mind. I sighed and made a quick sketch of it. It was hard to walk away.

"It'll be here. It's not going anywhere. We'll have more time to come back and study it," said Sie.

"OK," I said taking a deep breath. T took off her glittery new ribbon and tied it to the cedar branch draped across the trail. It was like roping off an archeological site or stretching DO NOT CROSS tape across a crime scene. This made me feel a little better.

"There! In the name of science," she said.

Suddenly I felt I was on my way to greatness.

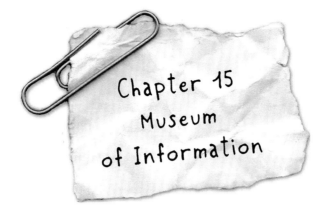

Chapter 15
Museum
of Information

I didn't tell Aunt Kitty about my discovery, because Sie was right—I should be sure first. The memory of the horse manure "bird nest" lingered as an ever-present reminder of that. When Aunt Kitty dropped us off at the hotel, Hunter was lounging in the shade chewing on the wooden leg of a lawn chair.

"We should have lunch out here, too," I said.

We brought out sandwiches, the twins' new books, and art stuff to laze in the shade. Tierra finished coloring her doll of Willy-Nilly. "I hardly remember what he looks like," she said, covering his paper body in glue and brown glitter.

COWPOKE WILLY

WILLY-NILLY'S
Camouflage Explorer Wear

In my field notebook, I sketched the tracks I had seen while they were fresh in my mind. I drew the deer and chipmunk's first—heart shapes and tiny handprints. Then I drew the strange three, four and five-toed tracks. I'd have to look these up later. I labeled date, time, and place where I found them. I was proud of my Wild memory and growing field note collection.

"I hope these tracks are clues to what that thing is," I said. I was still anxious about not bringing it back. "Aunt Kitty has her snake walk there tomorrow. Maybe we can go back and use the Scientific Method on it."

"OK, but no more snake talk, Holly," said T. Her Willy doll dried in the sun as she flipped through her new book.

"Wow, the dinosaurs your Aunt Kitty was talking about are mentioned in here. The lakes were deep enough for them to live in. Here's that snake-like one. It has a 40-foot long neck. That could be Charlie's giant snake monster."

BEACH BUM Life

reading + refreshment = relaxation

Mom and Boy strolled back from town. "I think I could really get into this island life," Mom said and yawned. She seemed changed on this vacation. Boy threw his pale, freckled arm around her and said, "Welcome to my world, Mom." He obviously had her under his black-clad, goth teen Boy spell.

"No cooking, no cleaning…" Mom mumbled. Boy was leading her to the beach as Gram and Aunt Kitty came back from their walk.

"I'm heading into town if you ladies want to go anywhere before dinner," Aunt Kitty announced.

"Library!" I said. "It's a museum of words and information."

"Maybe it's air conditioned," said T, pushing back her bangs. It had gotten hotter.

"Yeah, I can check the weather on the Internet there," said Sie. "We could use a storm to cool us off." The hotter it got, the happier we were that Aunt Kitty's car had air.

The library was a circular, wood-beamed building. "Wow! This must be what it looks like inside a beaver lodge," I said.

"And it has air conditioning," said T, collapsing in a chair. I scanned the room; the coast was clear. No sign of Ivy.

Sierra wandered over to the computers. I had just pulled out my field notes and sketches when Sie came back. "The Internet's down, but the librarian says big storms are supposed to hit here Thursday— the day of the picnic."

"Good to know. I'm going to find a book on animal tracks," I said. I went up to the help desk, where a scruffy-bearded, bed-headed guy in a green shirt was leaning over the counter to whisper to the librarian.

Whispering always alerts my Wild senses. It means secret information is about to be revealed. I pretended to look at the bin of sale books so I could eavesdrop. To make it look good, I bought a book on Michigan Indian legends with the 80 cents I had found earlier. Then I rushed back to report to the girls.

"Team! I overheard that bearded guy over there at the desk. He

said Sally is missing. He told the librarian to keep her eyes and ears open. And the creepy part is they want to keep it quiet and not start a panic in town!"

"Do you think someone kidnapped Sally?" Tierra gasped.

"I don't know. The guy said, 'Poor Sally, the cold-blooded old girl came up missing.'"

"We haven't seen her zipping about lately," said Sierra, chewing her pencil. "But why would she leave with the artist's party tomorrow?"

"It's no secret that folks are angry with her." I said, looking around. "People don't like having their homes messed with. With Sally bringing changes here, someone may want to get rid of her. Remember, King Strang was 'done in' by an angry mob when he brought change to the island. Queen Sally may be in real danger."

"First Willy-Nilly, and now Sally," said Tierra, wide-eyed.

"For an unhurried, unspoiled island there sure is a lot happening. Here one moment, gone the next. Beaver Island is changing fast," whispered Sierra.

Right then a man and woman burst through the library doors.

Both were in khaki garb with binoculars dangling from their necks. Both were out of breath. "We," the man gasped, "my wife and I, just saw some big thing swimming and splashing around in Fox Lake."

"We were watching a pair of common loons when it began thrashing nearby. It was huge," the woman said, fanning herself. "Big, yellow eyes, long body. Dreadful. It was no fish." The girls

and I looked at each other.

"Please keep your voices down," the librarian calmly said to the couple.

"Just this morning I talked to a fisherman who said he saw something like that," said a white-haired man, looking over his newspaper. "Said it was huge, serpent-like. Maybe old King Strang is getting revenge by sending the king of the serpents in." He chuckled and went back to reading his paper.

"Now Harold, everyone's been acting funny from the heat these days," said the librarian. "No snake monster here. Our snakes may be big but are harmless—to people anyway."

Tierra groaned. "Why must everyone remind me of how many rodent-eating snakes there are here?" Sierra patted her shoulder and we got up to leave.

"This is sounding more and more like Charlie Bird's story," I said, looking over the old book I had bought. Maybe stories can hold clues.

After all, Charlie did say that sometimes stories are not just stories.

Chapter 16
Wednesday:
Snakes and More
SNAKES!

It was hard to sleep—between the humidity, dreams of snakes, and thinking about the creepy thing on the lakeshore, I was awake most of the night. I couldn't get it out of my head. It was calling me. What was it? We had to find out today.

I managed to pull myself away from the fan and T's cooling spritzer bottle and slogged into the kitchen. I collapsed into a chair, my legs sticking to the seat. I looked in on Kenny, who was paler than ever. I hoped Aunt Kitty could look at him after her snake lecture today. He needed his color back soon, the judging was in two days!

Gram was putting yogurt into the fridge. She must've done her shopping early because of the heat. "Hear anything about Sally Sonnschein in town?" I asked casually.

Gram thought for a moment. "Sally? Nope. Everyone's too hot and crabby to gossip. It's gonna be another sizzling scorcher today."

The twins and I had breakfast outside. Hunter was sitting in a toddler's blow up pool in the shade. He was lapping up water surrounded by happy blue dolphins. I was surprised he hadn't popped it and eaten it yet, but it was still early.

"Not much better out here. No breeze," said T, pushing her bangs back. Hunter stood and shook his floppy ears, drenching us in warm dog water. It actually felt pretty good if you didn't think about it.

We were tossing him our soggy bagels when Gram came out. "Kitty said I could take you girls on a circle tour of the island," she said.

"An air-conditioned tour sounds great!" said T.

Sierra was excited to shoot pictures of island life. First on the list was Protar's tomb. Protar was a kindly "doctor" and local Beaver Island hero, unlike the greedy King Strang. Next we were going to stop at the bio school, but it was busy with students, so we went on to a beach full of terns and then stopped at the lighthouse at the tip of the island.

aka: Beaver Head Light

Beaver Island Lighthouse

Stone Circle

Protar's Tomb

"Doctor" Protar
(rubbing from tomb)

By noon we arrived at Miller's Marsh to look for beavers. The mosquitoes were so thick we decided no beaver in his right mind would come out, so we cut the visit short. Besides, yesterday's commotion at the library had us nervous around the water.

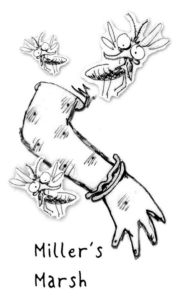

To make things worse, snakes were everywhere today making Tierra jumpy. After we stopped to move the third snake out of the road, she decided to stay in the car the rest of the tour, even after Gram told her that the snakes would be heading for cooler places in the heat of the day.

Miller's Marsh

Our last stop was the island's mysterious stone circle. Sierra snapped pictures of the big rocks hidden in the tall ferns.

"Who do you think put the stones here?" I asked.

"Maybe aliens," Sierra joked, wiggling her fingers like antenna on her head.

"When I was a kid, I remember hearing legends of flying ships around here," Gram said. "When folks can't quite explain certain things, they come up with all kinds of stories." At that moment the deafening roar of an airplane made us all duck as it skimmed over the treetops.

"What was that you said about flying objects?" Sie asked, laughing.

"I forgot, the airport's not far from here," said Gram, leaning against the boulder to rest. She placed a pebble in a carved out bowl in the stone. "I've often wondered what the purpose of these rocks were."

"These rocks are like an outdoor museum!" I said, feeling its rough surface.

"Well girls, time to go. It's getting late," said Gram.

"That's it! I bet this is a clock or calendar. Like Aunt Kitty said, you ask questions, think of guesses, then prove it," I said, taking notes on the rocks. I'd made my guess, but I'd have to prove it some other time.

We arrived at Fox Lake and Gram pulled lemonades out of the cooler. "You girls can cool off at the shore while I go look for Kitty's group," Gram said, heading around the lake.

"Let's go," I said. "Now's our chance to go study that gross, creepy thing."

Tierra looked nervous. "I don't know, with all the snakes out today. Your grandma did say they'd move into the shade, and it's shady in the cedars."

"It's like Charlie's story. The king of the snakes is calling them," Sie teased.

"Don't say that," Tierra said, cringing.

We headed down the cedar trail, past the place of turtle eggs and fishing lures, to where the trail narrowed. I smelled that same smell again. It was vaguely familiar, with a hint of—horse manure! There waved T's glittery ribbon, proudly marking the spot.

"It's still here," I sighed with relief. My scientific discovery claim to fame. Holly H. Wild, citizen scientist extraordinaire. I liked the sound of that. I had chills—and not because it was cooler in the cedars.

"I still think it's a dead person's arm. Look at the scars where leeches sucked out all the blood." Sie pointed out the football-shaped marks. "It looks like someone cut it off—or bit it in half."

"What if it's—Sally's arm?" whispered Tierra.

"Holy Creeps, times ten. I never thought about that," I said staring at the thing. It kinda started looking like an arm to me now, too. The woods suddenly seemed dark and scary.

"I guess there's only one way to tell," I said. "We have to get scientific on it!"

CREEPY THING CHOICES

OR

CHOOSE
ONE!

Giant Snake   Arm of Sally
--------   --------

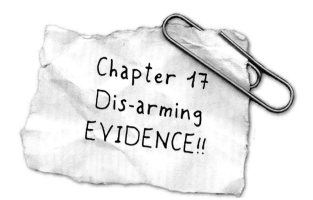

Chapter 17
Dis-arming
EVIDENCE!!

"Team Wild, fellow GeEKs, we are about to use the Scientific Method," I said, pulling my hat down. This time Sie had her camera and she started shooting pictures.

"We'll sketch it and measure it like they do on TV," I said, getting

Date: July 22

Place: Beaver Island, Fox Lake
Weather: Really, super, hot.
          Crazy super humid.

Size: About 13 inches long, 4 inches thick.
Color: Brownish
Texture: Smooth with bumps. Squishy.

Description: Lots of blood sucking marks from hundreds of leeches. OK, facts only, Scale-like football-shaped scars with tiny pores.

out my tools and notebook. As GeEK secretary, T took notes, while Sie and I worked over the strange, wrinkly thing.

We had gotten very scientific on it, but weren't finished yet. There was one last GeEK task left to perform. I poked it with a stick.

A good poking stick is essential to explorers. It allows you to examine gross things from a safe distance without actually touching them. It is the perfect tool for turning and flipping unknown finds of the creepy kind.

NEVER POKE anything LIVING!

POKING POINTERS

A poking stick can:
• dig, move or pry
• knock things down
• measure stuff
• flip smelly things

I poked it and waited for a reaction. What I got was T squealing. The "thing" only made a squooshy, watery sound.

"Don't, Holly!" pleaded Tierra. "What if it is Sally's arm? That's so rude."

"*If* it's Sally's arm," I said. "I still think it's a section of an ancient snake."

"Whether it's Sally's arm or part of a snake," said Sie, "whatever left it here might come back." Holy creeps, I never thought about that!

Tierra was looking at something in the ferns when a loud, smacking SPLASH hit the water.

"Let's get outta here!" T yelled. I fell backwards into Sierra, who tripped on a cedar knee. I was blinded by a bright flash as her camera hit the ground and bounced across the trail. Sie scooped it up and we both scrambled to our feet and took off after T, who was already halfway down the trail.

Out of breath from the run and shaken from the frightening loud splash at the lake, we were sure glad to see Aunt Kitty. When we collapsed into the cool car she handed us icy sodas.

"Aunt Kitty," I huffed, "what can you tell us about this island? I mean those giant snakes you told us about. They were real, but that was long ago, right?"

"Well, Holly, actually some exciting news has recently come in. Island biologists are finding giant herps here!"

I gulped. "Like what exactly?"

"Toads the size of squirrels! Snakes bigger than anything seen elsewhere in Michigan. They have larger heads so that they can eat those large toads," she giggled. She could really be gruesome when she wanted to be. T looked ill.

"Islands are like natural laboratories, kind of a big aquarium," she continued. "They have boundaries and are isolated. Because of

that and the fact that there are fewer enemy species, things live longer and so get bigger. This is found most with herps—the amphibians and reptiles."

"Oh, great," T moaned.

We rode back to the hotel in silence with our clothes sticking to us. When we finally got back to the hotel we dropped in front of the fan in our room while Sierra downloaded photos onto her laptop.

"Now what do we do?" muttered T.

"Well, we need to find out what made that splash," I said, sitting up.

"Hey, look at this. The camera took this when it fell," Sie said, staring at the screen. The photo had mud splatters, but between the

grasses and clumps of weeds in the water there were definitely two, big yellow eyes staring at us.

"Holy creeps, guys!" I said. "That's a reptile."

"Maybe it's a

beaver," Tierra said hopefully. Sie magnified the picture and printed it out.

"This has scales. Mammals have fur." I pointed to the long body. The long, spiky neck curved into the water. "The Island Snake Monster. It's back." I looked up at the girls.

Tierra grabbed her new book and flipped to the page on ancient sea creatures. "There!" she pointed at the picture titled *King Lizard*. "I just finished the chapter on early Michigan dinosaurs."

"Wow!" I said. "If this island lake has giant snakes and toads, imagine what could be living in Lake Michigan, one of the largest lakes in the world. This is exciting!"

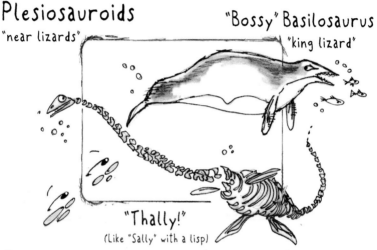

Plesiosauroids
"near lizards"

"Bossy" Basilosaurus
"king lizard"

"Thally!"
(Like "Sally" with a lisp)

Thalassomedon was a plesiosaur--not a dinosaur. It was a marine reptile, "lord of the seas", that lived in the ocean and breathed air! 40' long, sharp teeth, snake-like neck. Holy creeps!

"But what if that reptile got Sally and that thing is her arm?" asked T.

"Or maybe that thing is another giant snake that got—done in," Sierra said, drawing her hand across her throat.

"Team, it's time to assemble our information and draw our conclusion," I said. The twins, known for their organizational skills, set to work. They cleared a space as I laid out clues.

Our notes, sketches of tracks, photos of the scaly arm-like thing, Tierra's illustrations of Charlie Bird's story, the library couple's story, a frightened loon—one by one, they were placed onto a poster board. The twins moved the pieces around arranging them, working over it like surgeons.

"Glitter pen!" Tierra stuck out her hand. "M&Ms. I think better with M&Ms."

"Glue stick. Permanent, acid-free," ordered Sie. I slapped supplies into their waiting hands and watched in awe. This is so why we're a team.

Then Sierra put down her glue stick. "It's done," she said and dropped before the fan.

I was not prepared for what I saw. Indeed, we had drawn and pasted our conclusion.

On the 18 x 24 inch poster board before me was a hideous, writhing beast. And like the giant island snake monster of legend, I could now clearly see what damage this beast could do.

"We are dealing with something disastrous here," Sie said.

"It's bigger than I thought," I said. "The very thing that could save this island could also destroy this island. *If* the reptile in your photo is a rare giant snake, it needs to be preserved."

"But *if* folks hear about this giant snake, they will be too scared to go outside and will want a huge indoor theme park. So what we need to do is go get the evidence and present our conclusion to the experts at the bio station," said Sie. We all looked at each other. We knew what we had to do.

"We must stop this beast before it spoils the picnic," said T.

"Or destroys the unspoiled, unhurried island," I said. "And therefore, we will all be heroes. Awesome, times ten."

"Big thing swimming and splashi
Big yellow eyes, a long body.
Dreadful. It was no fish!"

Long ago, when the earth was new and the ar
was out naming the plants and animals. He ca
behind you. A giant snake, the King of Serpe
water killing all the animals. Manabozho told
refused. So Manabozho did what he had to do
serpent crawled out of the water. Manabozh
I could get a shot at him I can save my frier
ange my shape." So he made himself a
hen the snake came out, he looked a
is Manabozzzho tryi   to trick me.'
ueezed. And he sque-e   d and squeee
usted. "It mussst be a   mp." So it cr
s human form. He dre   s ash bow wit
ew true and hit it   ." But it didr
nto the water hissi   Manabozho,
nd with that,   gre   floo
But, Mana zho   quid   e cl
ends to   ney w

"Revenge by
sending the **king**
of the serpents"

CONCLUSION:

nd trees could talk. Our hero Manabozho

. large beautiful lake, the same one you see

ed there and had been coming out of the

ake, "Stop killing my friends." But the snake

nted the snake with his bow. Each time the

shoot. And Manabozho would miss! "If only

en Manabozho had an idea. "I am Manabozho,

ne stump and sit himself right by the

nd saw the stu "I'll jussst bet that

snake wrapped himself nd the stump

with all his might. The s came

ff to the water." Mana

asper tipped oak ar

the snake, it only

ing to kill you a

me upon the ear

down a great ceda

saved.

"We're ba-a-ck!"

missing
.Sally →

MONSTER?

The day of the Herp Picnic was so hot it was hard to peel our bodies away from the fan. By noon we had managed to drag ourselves into town. From the ice cream shop to the Print Shop Museum, people gossiped about island events.

Tourists buzzed like mosquitoes about the mysterious lake sightings. Fishermen discussed approaching storms. Islanders whispered about Sally Sonnschein missing the island's artist party the night before. Tempers boiled, stories bubbled. The hotter the weather got, the hotter the conversation became.

"Look at everyone," said Sierra. "It's island mayhem."

"Holly, we need to tell your Aunt about the creepy thing we found at the lake—she's giving her reptile talk there today," said T. "With all those people there, that's like setting bait for out the monster." Right then Snake-Boy came out the side door of the school. He hopped on his bike and headed toward town.

"I wonder if he knows what's going on," Sierra said as he rode away.

"Let's follow him," I said.

By the time we got to the corner he had disappeared, but smelly Mr. Buckthorn was standing there, fumbling with a dripping ice cream cone and talking to a well-dressed, wealthy-looking couple.

The tanned couple, in their matching sunglasses, white shorts and navy golf shirts, didn't look very happy.

"We lost him," Sie groaned.

Buckthorn popped the rest of the ice cream cone into his mouth as the couple walked away. In all of the excitement I had completely forgotten about Ivy. Maybe the monster got her, too.

"Did you see a kid run by?" I asked Mr. Buckthorn.

"Haven't seen anyone. I've been busy doing business," he said, jingling coins in his pocket. "Well, gotta run. Time is money." He pulled a green onion out of his pocket. "Diet," he said as he crunched and hurried away.

"Must be the seafood diet, he eats everything he sees," joked Sierra.

We heard a car honk. "Girls! Over here!" It was Aunt Kitty. "Good news, girls, good news! I finished the Herp Hike and it's time for the picnic! Your mom and Gram are already there getting things set up." Hunter stuck his big, white head and floppy, brown ears through the window. Ugh!

At the lake, Aunty Kitty carried her fluffy Green Bean-Pineapple-Sunrise-Surprise Salad to the big tent. People were setting up chairs and tables and bringing in coolers of food. Mom and Gram were in the back, fanning themselves with turtle-shaped paper plates. Boy was helping a guy hang a sign that read "Happy Herping One and All!"

"If they only knew," I sighed, "that the biggest herp ever is lurking out there." We grabbed icy sodas and some of Aunty Kitty's Lavender Herbed Lemon Cookies. Hey, these weren't too bad!

Tierra squirmed around. "Ouch," she uttered. She pulled a silver necklace out of her pocket.

"Holy creeps, T! Where'd you get that?" I asked, spewing lavender cookie crumbs.

"Oh! I found it yesterday on the shore by the ferns, before the splash. In all the excitement I totally forgot about it. Maybe it can be my new good luck charm," she said, grinning.

"That's no charm, Tierra, that's Sally's necklace," I said, studying the pendant's design. "See?" I pointed at it. "It's a sun with an 'S' in the center."

"It looks like a turtle to me," shrugged Tierra.

"I don't know about the design, but I do know that I saw her wearing it the other night at the pub. I have Wild memory, remember?" I said, tapping my hat.

"If it belongs to Sally, how could she have gotten her chair down there? The path is pretty muddy and narrow," said Sie.

"I don't know that either. But finding your good luck charm may mean bad luck for Sally," I said.

"Holly, we need to go get that creepy thing," said Sierra, "and bring it back to your Aunt Kitty, *now*. People are starting to arrive. And from the looks of those dark clouds in the west I estimate that the storms will be here by 1:00 p.m. The temperature has already peaked at 95 degrees." She checked her key chain thermometer.

"They're miles away," I said, "We're fine. We won't be that long."

Right then Boy came up to us. "Mom says the three-legged, four-toed salamander sack race and frog meet will start soon," he said. "Later, they're bringing out snakes. I hope they have a cobra. Dude, that would be sweet." Then he sauntered back to the food line.

That's where I saw the Buckthorns. Mrs. B. was fanning herself and Queenie while Mr. B. was speaking with the wealthy couple again. Ivy was behind them. I guess she wasn't eaten after all.

"Snake-Boy," pointed Sie. Behind the couple was the boy in the raggedy shirt. He moved toward the chair where the woman's purse hung and stuck his hand inside.

"He's stealing again! Hey, kid!" I yelled.

The boy looked up at us and suddenly made a mad dash down for the lake, disappearing through the cedars.

A gust of wind picked up our hair and sent green turtle plates rolling. Sierra sniffed the air, licked her finger and held it up. "It's time," she announced. "We have fifteen minutes before this storm hits."

"You really are something, Sierra Hills," I said, pulling down my hat.

"Thank you. It's a gift. But we must hurry."

Chapter 19
Museum Week
MAYHEM!

We sped down the trail after Mr. Sneaky Snake-Boy, but didn't see him anywhere. The sky was the color of Aunt Kitty's fluffy, fruity, green bean salad.

"We lost him again," I said.

"Forget him, we have to hurry!" Sie charged on.

The three of us ran through the tangle of branches. We found the tree where Tierra's pink ribbon beckoned us from the branch. On the path near the water lay the gross, withered creepy thing.

"Hurry, this weather looks unstable," Sierra said. She reached into her pocket and snapped out their rain ponchos. In an instant, the two were clad head to toe in flapping, yellow vinyl.

"Huh, it's really quiet," I

said. The woods and the water were still. Not a branch moved. No peeping birds or chirping chipmunks. I pulled out my poking stick and a plastic grocery bag. Then a gust of wind hit us, whipping trees and rocking them side to side.

"Hurry, Holly," whined Tierra, her voice drowned out by a rumble of thunder. The storm was now quickly approaching.

Turning my hat around backwards to concentrate, I pushed and prodded the creepy thing until I had rolled it to the mouth of the plastic bag that Sierra held open. Water oozed out both ends.

"Are you done?" Tierra asked, looking as green as the sky.

Thunder rumbled like a huge rock rolling our way.

"Do it, Holly," said Sierra, grimacing. "It's going to get real ugly—real soon."

With one final move, I flipped it into the bag. Lightning flashed, thunder shook the shore, and a lone loon yodeled on the lake.

"You angered its spirit!" Tierra wailed. Sierra dropped the bag and the twins hit the trail running like two yellow ghosts flying through the trees as the icy downpour hit.

The lake was as dark as the clouds rolling above it. Frothy waves slammed the shore. Someone's rowboat anchored on the lake was tossed about like a toy. Sierra's storm had hit. My watch carabineer flashed *1:00*. Holy creeps, the girl's good.

Sierra and Tierra were still screaming when I caught up with them. I didn't know if they were screaming because the green sky was collapsing upon us and the rain was pelting us or if it was because I was right behind them with the creepy thing in the sack.

Whether it was part of a giant snake monster or Sally's arm, I was glad I had collected it before the storm had swept it away. I imagined headlines and a picture of me holding the thing in the bag.

By the time we got back to the tent, the storm had marched on. Kids were throwing hail the size of Junebugs at each other. Fortunately, the cedars had protected us from being pelted senseless. A worried Mom, Gram, and Aunt Kitty met us at the trail head. All eyes were fixed on Team Wild.

A wide-eyed Ivy stood next to her wide-eyed father. Totally drenched and dripping wet, I held up the plastic bag.

"I found it," I announced loudly, the bag swinging in front of me.

Once again, Ivy demonstrated the blood-curdling scream that had greeted us the moment we dropped anchor on the island a mere five days ago.

"She's got it in that bag!" Ivy roared in her foghorn voice, pointing at me. "Kill it Daddy! Don't let it get me!"

That's all it took for the entire group to react like a herd of stampeding buffalo.

Panicked picnickers bolted out of the tent and onto tables. Screaming kids scrambled onto whatever chairs hadn't tipped over. Babies wailed like the sirens that should've gone off before the storm hit. The kilt-clad Highland Herpers Bagpipe Band leaped atop the drum set on the bandstand, their pipes droning eerily like a dying goose.

There I stood in silence—left holding the bag.

Thanks to Ivy, it seemed that I, Holly H. Wild, now had everyone's attention. One wheezy bagpipe note floated through the air as Aunt Kitty stepped forward, calm and tiny. The only sound was that of the tent flapping and snapping in the post-storm breeze.

Mr. Scruffy-Beard-Bed-Head guy from the library stood next to Aunt Kitty. It was too quiet. Much like the calm before that storm that had just swept through.

"We'll take that bag, young lady," he said, carefully taking it from me.

"It's dead," I said. The crowd gasped and backed up. Sierra and Tierra stood on the sidelines watching while I stood shivering in the middle of the tent with five hundred eyes upon me—me and the bagged creepy thing.

"It's evidence," I said to Aunt Kitty. "We found a part of a giant snake monster by the lake," I said. "Or it might be someone's arm," I added. Another gasp went up from the crowd. The buffalo prepared to charge again. I chewed on my thumbnail and sweat rolled down my back. Or maybe it was melting hail.

"This is Chase Fieldman, a biologist here on the island," said Aunt Kitty. Chase reached inside and pulled out the creepy thing, slapping it onto the table with a loud sloppy, squishy *shplat*. Bubbles gurgled out and plipped as he rolled the thing over on its side with a sloppy, sucking sloosh.

He played with his scruffy chin and was quiet for a moment. Rainwater dripped off the tent. I hoped that the thoughtful silence meant that this was one amazing discovery and he was in total shock and disbelief that I had collected the disgusting, slimy thing before him.

"Holly, you've found a fine specimen of *Nuphar luteum*," Aunt Kitty said with a warm, elfin smile. She poked the thing with her finger. Someone handed her a microphone and the loud speaker crackled. This was it—my hero moment!

"Really?!?" I squeaked. Whatever Aunt Kitty had just said sure sounded amazing.

"It was once called 'pine snake' by the indigenous peoples here in the Great Lakes region," Aunt Kitty said, addressing the group. "However, the name is misleading." There seemed to be a very...long...pause. "For it is neither a pine tree nor a snake. In fact, folks call it 'pine snake' because it looks like both."

"So, what are you saying exactly?" I croaked. My voice caught in my throat like it was snagged on the red spoon lure I found—the one with all the rusty hooks.

"A common water weed," said Aunt Kitty into the microphone. "The native yellow pond lily, often referred to as 'spatterdock.' This is its rhizome, which is an underground stem with roots that can grow over six feet long. The plant is excellent cover for turtles, fish, and snakes."

"A weed?" said Tierra and Sierra simultaneously. Their jaws dropped and they stared at me like I knew all along. Like I should have known. Like it was horse manure. The word seemed to float and swirl around my brain like a leaf in a whirlpool—in front of two hundred and fifty people.

The hero moment I imagined earlier lay melting at my feet, like the piles of dissolving hail. A redheaded kid in yellow sunglasses sneered at me.

"Oh," I said, deflating like a balloon. I'm happy that Aunt Kitty's a plant expert, but I wasn't really interested in hearing its natural history at this time—in front of everyone—on a loudspeaker. My cheeks and freckles sizzled.

"...muskrats and beavers are especially fond of eating the rhizomes, while ducks and geese relish its seeds." Aunt Kitty droned on like the bagpipes.

"PINE SNAKE!" or Yellow Pond Lily

sun's energy

FOOD and SHELTER for:

- beavers
- muskrats
- ducks
- fish
- turtles

oxygen

"But the scars on it," I noted. "It's not someone's arm?"

"An arm?" Chase said, taking over the mike from Aunt Kitty. "No, I'm quite sure. The spatterdock is very much a plant. The rhizome can get as long and thick as an arm. The scars are from where the leaves were once attached. They send oxygen, blah, blah, blah…" he went on as the speaker crackled in the background.

But I didn't hear anything else after that. That dizzy, oogey, sick-to-my-stomach-from-too-many-candy-bars feeling had come back again—times ten.

Chapter 20
Here There Be MONSTERS!

By now, everyone had climbed down from the chairs and tables and returned to their groups, whispering to each other and straightening things up.

"Soooo, what you're saying is, this is *not* a monster, *not* a snake, and *not* the arm of poor, old Sally?" I asked weakly. Chase gasped. A fork clanged loudly in an empty glass casserole dish.

"Sally!" he exclaimed. It got quiet again in the tent. "What do you know about Sally? We've been looking for her." He stroked his scraggly beard faster.

I had everyone's attention again. This time the girls stepped in. We told Chase the story about the lures, the path, the splashing, and the yellow eyes. We showed them the sketches of the tracks, the eggshells, Sierra's photos, and the pictures in Tierra's book. Everything spilled out like a big, gushing rush of water being dumped from a pail.

When we were done and all had been said I asked, "So what the heck is down on the lake shore?"

"I don't know. We should investigate. Show us where you found this," Chase said.

A loud **BANG** came from the back as Mr. Buckthorn barreled out of the tent. In his haste he had flipped the salad table, depositing

Aunt Kitty's Green Bean-Pineapple-Sunrise-Surprise Salad onto the laps of Ivy, her mother and their yapping poodle. Slimed again, times three.

Tierra, Sierra, and I guided the party down the trail through the dripping cedars. Gram, Mom, and Chase followed as a baying Hunter dragged Aunt Kitty along.

I spotted Tierra's soggy, non-glittery, pink ribbon hanging limply over the trail, when suddenly my feet went out from under me. I had found the same knobby cedar knee that Sierra had.

There was a muffled crack as I landed. Breaking in two, my poking stick had poked its last poke. I felt really sick inside. Hunter, whining and white-eyed, stopped and backed up the trail.

Two things came to mind. First, I have to remember never to trip over this cedar root, ever again. The second thing was a memory of the glittering, yellow eyes from the photo on Sierra's laptop. Because right now, laying in the mud and covered with muck, I was face to face with those very same metallic eyes.

When I fell, my hands had instinctively flown out and grabbed onto the snout of the yellow-eyed beast. This was a good thing—I was holding its jaws shut. I wondered if this was what it was like when Great Aunt Daisy Crockett leaped onto the bear for her brother.

Then it dawned on me, I was holding a real live monster! In all of Gram's Wild women stories, no one had ever wrassled a monster before. I would've heard about that. I, Holly H. Wild, was the first!

I was peering into its golden eyes, when it squirmed and whipped its long tail, delivering a sting to my cheek. Holy creeps! It would be all right by me if it didn't do *that* again. I wrapped my hands tighter around the long snout of many sharp teeth.

Suddenly, Snake-Boy appeared out of nowhere. He dropped down onto the writhing, twisting beast, holding its clawed feet and

long tail still. That's when I noticed that the poor thing was chained to a tree by a pink leash.

"Thanks!" I grunted, relieved not to get another tail lashing.

"Holly!" yelled Aunt Kitty and Gram.

"Sally!" Chase shouted as he made his way through the dripping branches, showering us with cold wetness again.

"Sally?" The girls and I echoed, as Snake-Boy and I struggled in the mud with the four-foot long beast. "Who's Sally?"

"This is Sally. Old Swamp-water Sally," said Chase. "That's what we call her at the bio station. It's a joke. Folks often mistake salamanders or "sallies" for reptiles, when they're really amphibians. Sally's a caiman, a reptilian relative of the alligator.

A "herp", but NOT a reptile.

Salamander

So as a joke we call her "Swamp-water Sally." She was an unwanted pet donated to us. She was supposed to be the star of the herp show today, but she mysteriously came up missing this week. We didn't want to start a panic and spoil Museum Week, so we've been quietly searching for the old girl."

"I thought Sally was the old woman in the wheelchair," I said.

"You thought Aunt Sally was Swamp-water Sally? That's so totally hilarious," said Snake-Boy.

"Your aunt?" I said, baffled. "Who are you?"

"I'm Robin Merriweather," Snake-Boy said, "and Sally Sonnschein's my Great-Aunt."

By now, the well-dressed couple in the matching sunglasses and many of the picnickers had filed down the trail.

"This reminds me of the time my Great-Aunt Daisy Crockett wrassled gators in the swamps of Florida," said Gram, telling the woman in sunglasses.

"We saw alligators in Florida," piped T and Sie.

"Those are wonderful stories," I said, not really thrilled about a bunch of strangers standing over my muddy butt while I held Sally, "but can someone help me? I'm really wet and kinda muddy."

"Oh, sure," Chase said. He took over for me as some bio station people ran up with one *huge* cooler.

"How did Old Sally get down here?" Chase asked, playing with his beard. The wriggling caiman was unchained and popped into the cooler.

"From the looks of this pink, jeweled collar I'd say a pet owner took her, Mr. Fieldman," I said. "There are lots of dogs on the island for the pet show."

"So you're not the thief that took her?" Sie questioned Robin, formerly known as Snake-Boy.

"Me, a thief? Never," Robin said.

"But the toy store candy," said T. "And that lady's purse," she pointed at the woman in sunglasses.

"That's my mom. She and my dad flew in yesterday," he said, blushing. "And as for the toy store thing, I went back later to pay. I was in a hurry," he said, shaking wet, muddy hair out of his eyes.

"Oh," I said, nodding. I understood. "I'm in a hurry sometimes, too." Sie coughed. "OK, most all the time."

Aunt Kitty was examining plant leaves on the trail. She popped them into her bag before scurrying over to us. "Now that Old Sally is safe, we can return to the picnic for a rousing reptilian feast," she announced. Hunter bayed at the mention of food.

I was hungry now, even though I was covered in muck and smelled like a blend of Boy's socks, the inside of Aunt Kitty's car, and green onions.

Back at the picnic, my embarrassment had worn off like most of the mud I had been caked in. Things had turned out OK and Robin was not a thief, but a really cool kid.

"You're all heroes!" Aunt Kitty beamed at us as she served us her Chocolate-Mint-Rosemary-Banana-Berry Cake. A botanist she was, a cook she was not. "You rescued Swamp-water Sally! Three cheers for you and your friends, Holly!"

"I don't understand. Why did you take the candy?" Sierra asked Robin as she picked rosemary leaves out of the frosting.

"It wasn't for me. It was for a snake," Robin said, turning bright red.

"What snake?" asked Tierra, pulling up her legs.

"Not here," he said. "A snake I found on the shore Monday, where we were today. I was trying to catch it to study it."

"But snakes don't eat candy," I said.

"It wasn't candy. It was a package of sunflower seeds," Robin explained.

"But snakes don't eat seeds, either," Sierra said.

"Precisely. It was a fox snake. They're *rodentivorous*, meaning they only eat mice and voles, small mammals. And rodents eat seeds. Rodents are kinda like nature's fast food."

"Thanks for reminding me," sighed T.

"Excuse me, young man. Did you say fox snake?" Aunt Kitty asked, nearly flipping a piece of her herbed concoction onto Gram.

"Yes," said Robin. "I like snakes. When I heard what that Buckthorn was going to do to my Aunt's property, I called my parents to come help talk her out of selling. But it's too late and Aunt Sally is gone. Buckthorn had her sign papers on Monday. She was so upset that she left. This means the indoor theme park will be built after all. Buckthorn plans on poisoning the water in the marsh to get rid of the insects and snakes, dynamiting the beaver lodges, and putting an asphalt parking lot over everything."

"Mr. Buckthorn is worse than Charlie's giant snake monster," Sierra whispered to me.

"Golly Goober, that's it!" I blurted. Aunt Kitty, Gram, Robin, and the girls looked at me. "Goober knows the world with his nose. I smelled green onions and Aunt Kitty picked up the leaves on the trail. I recognized them and their smell. Mr. Buckthorn is the one who took Sally and staked her out there on Queenie's leash." Just like Manabozho, my arrow hit the mark this time.

"No one shtaked me anywhere," came a voice from the rear of the tent. "But he *vas* the von who talked me into selling my land."

Behind us stood Sally Sonnschein. Out of her chair, leaning on a cane, she had twigs and leaves poking out of her hair. Her elegant clothes were replaced with a paint-stained denim jacket over a white blouse and khaki shorts. For being unkempt, she still looked regal.

"That's right, Old Sally's back. Chair!" she ordered. Charlie pulled up a chair and wiped potato salad off of the seat.

"Aunt Sally, what happened to you?" asked Robin. "Were you kidnapped?"

"Ach! Nein. No, no, silly boy," Sally waved her hand. "I've been in the vilds this veek. Painting." Charlie handed her a lemonade. "Sank you, Charlie."

"After I signed avay my land and took that man's down payment I could not live wis myself. I could not bear the cold shoulder I vas getting in town. Ach! Alvays I move too quickly. I vanted to shlow down and shmell the roses," Sally said, shaking her head.

"So I got up and valked along the shore. I said to myself, *'It's so beautiful here.'* The flowers, the birds, the vater. Suddenly, I had a change of heart. I changed my mind. Vat a fool I vas to sell!" Sally pounded the table.

"I vanted to see my cabin for zhe last time. I hadn't been there in years. I vas loading my rowboat ven I heard shplashing. A big shnake? I vas afraid. I hopped in and rowed avay to my cabin. Ven I got zhere I loved it. I shttayed all veek. Painting shlowly, valking shlowly. No vrooming in my chair. Zhis island, zhis lake, they shlow you down. I forgot zhat. Ven the shtorms vere over I came back to tell you I vas safe and sound."

"I'm glad you had a good time," Charlie said, patting her hand gently with his big paw.

"Sank you, Charlie. But it's too late. Zhis beautiful unshpoiled, unhurried island vill be kaput. Deshtroyed. Shpoiled. Ach! Vat have I done?" she said, sinking into her chair. "Vat can I do to save my precious lake? I looked everywhere for a rare plant, a flower, anysing that might save my land from being deshtroyed. Our land," she said, patting Robin's hand.

"Robin, tell me about the fox snake," said Aunt Kitty. "Beaver Island has green snakes, garter snakes, ring-necked and red-bellied snakes, northern water snakes and milk snakes—but no fox snakes. Are you certain?"

"I saw it twice. With Buckthorn's plans to push out the snakes, I wanted to catch it and move it to a safer home," he said.

"When was the last time you saw this snake?" asked Aunt Kitty.

The Snakes of Beaver Island

garter snake

green snake

fox snake

"This morning. But the storm ruined my plan," Robin said, wiping his frosting-covered hands on his shorts. He might be really smart, but he was still a kid.

"So we don't have real evidence that it was a fox snake," said Aunt Kitty, poking at crumbs on her turtle plate. She sighed one great, big, Beaver Islander sigh.

ring-necked snake

red-bellied snake

northern watersnake

milk snake

Chapter 22
Changes for the Good Are Better

The storm brought cooler weather, which brought happier moods. The music, food, and games continued. More importantly, Robin and I got dry clothes. Everyone, including both Sallys, enjoyed themselves after the day of rain and excitement. Sally the caiman looked like a happy herp with her fish dinner. Sally the artist chatted with islanders, trying to come up with a plan to save their unspoiled, unhurried home.

Robin introduced us to his Aunt Sally. "So young ladies, you sought someone did me in and I vas floating about the lake. That shtory makes me laugh and I vill never live down zhat name." She chuckled softly. "I am lucky to have such good friends and family. As for that shmelly Buckthorn, he's the real schnake in the grass." She shook her fist, her bracelets jangling. "I vill not stop until I get my land back. I vill find a vay! I am Sally Sonnschein, Artist-of-Change!"

"Miss Sonnschein," said Tierra, "I found this on the shore."

"Ach! My necklace! Sank you child. I sought it vas lost forever." Sally squeezed Tie's hand. We went back to the car where Gram, Mom, Boy, and Aunt Kitty waited.

"You know Holly, Daisy didn't wrassle gators til she was thirteen," Gram said, winking. "You beat her on that one."

"You don't need to go far to have Wild adventures," said Aunt

Kitty. She removed a pin from her vest. "For you, Holly, for your own collection." It was a tiny alligator pin.

"Thanks, Aunt Kitty," I said, pinning it onto my hat. I was happy, but still felt like I had let down the island. My discovery was not rare. The herps, plants, and other animals were still in danger of losing their home.

"I almost forgot, Holly. Your bio-fact." Aunt Kitty handed me the white plastic bag.

"It's too squishy to take home. I say, release it back into the wild for the next tourist to discover, or for a beaver to snack on."

Back at the hotel, Boy and Robin camped out on the beach for the night while I helped the girls get the art projects ready for the show.

"So monsters really are real," said Sierra, printing out pictures on Aunt Kitty's portable printer. "Buckthorn's going to change the island into a mall of frenzy. Like we don't have enough of those. He's going to strangle the island with asphalt, dynamite, poison, and fertilizer—all for his theme park."

"Guys, we still need to stop him," I said, polishing my new pin. "Nothing's changed."

"Give it up, Holly. We're done being heroes. You nearly got your hand chomped off. Sally's home and Buckthorn will be fined big time for what he did. Be happy," said Sierra.

"And your hypothesis was correct. Mr. B. was the herp-napper who took the caiman," said T.

"You linked Buckthorn's habit of chewing green onions to the leaves that your Aunt Kitty found. His bad breath gave him away. OK, that and they found Queenie's name on the leash. He's not the brightest beast on the block," Sie said.

"Buckthorn is one beastly monster I want to see stopped," T said. "My new book says monsters come out when it's time for people to pay attention. When it's time for a change, they scare people into action. It's up to the islanders now."

"I suppose," I said. Sie glued the last photo to the poster board. She held it up. It looked spectacular.

"I just wanted to discover something. I wanted to help the islanders—and I wanted to see a real, live beaver. And now I need a new poking stick, since mine broke. Good sticks are hard to find," I said, slumping in a heap.

"Cheer up, Holly, GeEKs never give up," Sie said. Both girls gave me a hug. As usual, Sie was right—I would not give up.

After breakfast the next morning, I went to check on Kenny. Aunt Kitty was stopping by to look him over. "Kenny!" I yelled. "Your skin came off!" I pulled out a four-foot long, transparent, sock-like skin. Boy and Robin came in.

"Sweet," said Boy, slurping milk from his cereal bowl. "Can I have it?"

"I'm gonna keep this one," I said, "but there will be more where that came from—you can have the next one. Now you'll win for sure, Kenny."

"Willy-Nilly would've won the pet show if Kenny hadn't murdered him," said Tierra. I winced.

"What do you mean murder?" Robin asked T.

"Kenny ate her hamster, Willy-Nilly," said Sie.

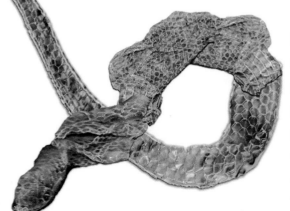

"I don't think Kenny ate your pet," said Robin. "When snakes are ready to shed their skin, they're nervous 'cause they can't see well, so they hide.

They don't eat before they shed. They eat *after* they shed," he explained.

"Now who's jumping to conclusions? I knew Kenny didn't eat him," I said, studying Kenny's hand-me-downs.

"Sorry I blamed Kenny for murdering Willy-Nilly in his sleep," she sighed.

"So where's Willy then?" I asked.

"Think like a hamster," said Boy, shrugging. All five of us kids started a room-to-room search. Pretty soon Boy yelped, "Hey, Tierra!"

In the living room, Boy pointed at his backpack on the floor. Carefully pulling back a shirt, he revealed a cozy nest in his bag and a very happy Willy. "Dude, you've been eating my corn chips," said Boy.

"Willy-Nilly," Sierra said, peeking inside, "isn't a Willy—she's a Wilma!"

"Huh?" Tierra asked, confused. There in Boy's wadded up black t-shirt, were five squirming, pink babies. Wilma stared up at us.

"Hamsterlets! He's a she!" Tierra said reaching for a baby, but Robin stopped her.

"Not yet, T, we have to carefully move them to safety," he instructed her. "I used to have hamsters," he said. "We can't disturb her when she has her babies, or she might hurt them."

Tierra came in with the hamster habitat. Robin slowly picked up the nest, t-shirt and all, and placed the family inside. When the lid snapped shut, we all sighed with relief.

"Everyone's home," smiled Sie.

"As for you young lady, no pet show for you," T said to Wilma.

"Oh well, you'll have to wait until the next pet show to wear your cowboy outfit."

"You can enter something else, T. You already have Willy—er—Wilma signed up," I said.

"You're right. I have my Willy doll," she said, grinning.

"Two more Museum Week mysteries solved. We'll need a vacation from our vacation," said Sie.

There was a tapping at the door. Elfish giggling came from the kitchen. "Hello, campers!"

"Hi Aunt Kitty, Gram. We're in here. Kenny's fine. He shed his skin," I said, dangling the scaly souvenir.

"That boy got too big for his britches," said Gram. Then we showed everyone the new hamster family.

"Won't your mother be surprised when you get back home," chuckled Mom.

"Home," I said glumly. "I forgot we have to leave."

"Well then, are you kids ready for one more adventure?" Aunt Kitty asked. "I thought we'd finally drive down to see the beaver lodges. My duties on the island are finished."

"Awesome!" I jumped up. "So there really are beavers on Beaver Island!"

Driving through town we watched people loading their luggage onto the docks. It was funny how many people we recognized after being here for only a few days. Everyone in town was in a better mood thanks to the cooler weather. This time as Sally whizzed by in her chair, she waved.

"By the way, Mr. Buckthorn claims he was borrowing

the caiman to chase Museum Week tourists away from his property. He insists that he thought it was an ugly dog," said Gram.

"That, I'd believe," laughed Sierra.

"He's closing the deal on the Sonnschein property today. And Mr. Merriweather, Robin's dad, has flown in a lawyer to look things over. We can only cross our fingers and hope," said Aunt Kitty.

When we got to the lake, the tent had been taken down and the tables and chairs carted away. Unfortunately, the bulldozer was still parked there, a big, ugly reminder of the island's fate.

"Hey, someone painted graffiti all over the Extra Extravaganza Park, Pool and Mini-Mall sign," said Sierra. It was covered with large orange and purple flowers, a big yellow sun and "STOP the Mall" scrawled in red.

"Can't imagine who'd do that," chuckled Gram.

The day was perfect, blue skies and a light breeze. It was nice to hike and not have your clothes stick to your skin. Museum Week was ending on a beautiful day.

Walking down the trail through the cedars, Aunt Kitty nodded toward a pointy stump and announced, "Here's a sign from a different builder. These are *beaver pencils*." Wood shavings from a beaver's nightly chores were scattered about.

"I wouldn't want to write with that," joked Sierra.

"I thought a person

chopped those with an axe," I said, picking up a wood chip. These were the very same ones T launched as boats a few day earlier. "And all this time, beaver clues were right here under my nose."

"Speaking of nose, that odor you smell is the beaver's scent mound. They build a mound of mud and wet leaves and mark it with their scent. It's a territory marker for keeping other beavers out."

"Hey, I smelled that! Beavers know the world through their noses, too—like Goober," I said. I had new respect for dog noses.

"If you look, listen, and smell, signs are everywhere. Beaver signs include tracks, felled trees, scent mounds, chews, and their splashing tail warning system."

"There's a lot to learn to be an explorer," I said, collecting some shavings.

"Every time you go outdoors you learn. The more you go, the more you know," said Aunt Kitty.

"Yeah. And I did find its favorite food," I said. "Pine snake."

"Nature's tricky. Being a naturalist means being a detective," said Aunt Kitty.

"And being curious," I said, then froze. Sunlight dappled the trail when my eagle eye noticed something near T's feet.

"Freeze, Tierra! Whatever you do—don't move," I said.

Aunt Kitty's eyes got as big as melons.

Tierra yelped. Coiled up right next to her neon-green-and-black-checkered sneakers was a thick-bodied, checkered reptile much longer than the one I had wrestled.

"Pine snake!" exclaimed Aunt Kitty. "No one move!" Tierra squeezed her eyes shut.

"That's no plant, that's the biggest snake I've ever seen in my life," I said.

Aunt Kitty leaned slightly to look at the snake. "Here is one red-headed Beaver Islander I'm happy to see. This Western Fox Snake, *Elaphe vulpina vulpina*, is often called a *'pine snake.'* They are called a Fox Snake for the odor they emit if disturbed because it smells musky, like a fox."

"I wish people could keep names straight," I groaned. "Names are so confusing."

"V-very f-funny," Tierra whispered, peeking out one eye. "Just don't let it sting me with its tongue."

"Snakes can't sting with their tongues. And they don't use their tongues for swallowing like we do. Snakes actually smell with their tongues," said Robin.

"Smell with their tongues," I said. "That's awesome." Between dogs and snakes I've learned a lot about smelling and how animals know their world.

"They flick their tongue out and taste the air, then bring it back inside their mouth where it touches something called Jacobson's organ. This tasting organ identifies the 'smell' as predator or prey."

"OK, guys I get it. I don't want it to hear you and bite me," said T, shivering.

"Snakes don't have ears that hear like ours, they feel vibration under their bellies. Stay still. It won't move," said Robin. This Robin was a wealth of snake information. We will have to make him a GeEK.

"This pine snake or western fox snake is found in the Upper Peninsula's pine forests. It's a distant northern relative of Kenny's.

See the Mickey-Mouse-ear pattern near its tail? That's how I know it's a fox snake," explained Aunt Kitty, pointing out the marking. Now that she mentioned it, it did look like Kenny.

"Michigan has two fox snake species, eastern and western. The eastern fox snake, *Elaphe vulpina gloydi,* lives in the Lower Peninsula and is listed as threatened species," she said.

FOX SNAKE
"mouse ear" spot
How ironic! You are what you eat?

"You mean like it's endangered?" asked T, peeking at it. "That it could be extinct someday, like the giant beaver?"

"Sadly, if precautions aren't taken, yes—it could become extinct," said Aunt Kitty.

"How can you tell the difference between the two?" I asked, eyeing the dozing snake.

"Western fox snakes have 40 or more dark blotches on their backs, while eastern fox snakes only have around 30," said Robin.

"Well, there are 42 to be exact," announced Tierra, looking down at her feet. "I like math."

"Hurray for you, Miss Tierra!" gushed Aunt Kitty.

"It is very pretty. And very large." T looked down at it again. "I do like his patterns and color scheme. It's a festive, reddish, fox-like color," she said smiling. "Actually, it's really very cool."

Sierra clicked a picture of the two. And just in time. The snake decided that this place was too busy for basking. Vibrating its tail in the leaves, it slithered off leaving its tracks in the mud.

"Good job, Sierra," Aunt Kitty said. "Taking pictures is best. Some people mistake them for a venomous snake and kill them out of fear. Others capture them illegally for the pet trade. This affects their population. And to make matters worse, their habitat is being destroyed." Suddenly, Aunt Kitty pulled out her phone and made a call. I could see that she was thinking Wild thoughts.

"Poor snakes getting pushed out of their homes," said Tierra. Sierra and I looked at her and laughed. "I had a change of heart," T shrugged. She was one brave GeEK.

"This western fox snake is not unusual enough to slow Buckthorn down. It would take a rare or threatened snake to stop his theme park plans," said Aunt Kitty, frowning and hanging up her phone.

"Holy creeps, why can't things turn out right?" I asked, feeling defeated. For a moment everything seemed hopeful. We were so close to saving the island.

Everybody headed back to the car. I wanted to go say goodbye to the beaver, the snake, the loon, and the lake. Taking one last look, I pulled the squishy rhizome from my bag and placed it on the shore.

"Maybe some hungry beaver will find you," I said and sighed. "Wait up guys," I called, running up the trail. That was when a cedar knee caught my toe—again.

Once more I tumbled into the mud. But something lying on top of the mud caught my eye. A long, slender stick. One gnawed by sharp teeth.

"Holy creeps! A real live beaver chew." I could hardly breathe as I picked it up. It was chiseled clean and white where the bark was stripped off. It could be a handy fishing pole or a spear for getting apples in the orchard. It fit my hand just right and would fit perfectly into my new-old explorer pack. I suddenly felt hopeful again. I wasn't giving up.

"I got two new tools from Beaver Island. The Scientific Method and a new poking stick!"

Covered in mud, I caught up to everyone and showed them my find.

"Naturalists learn about the natural world by poking it with a stick," I said. "And us kids are closer to the ground than adults. We see a lot more, and smell a lot more."

POKING STICK POWER

Michigan beaver-made

× 10!

"And you do spend more time closer to the ground and smell more than anyone I know, Holly," teased Sierra.

"It's all in the name of science," I said, grinning.

Chapter 25
Change of Plans

We were piling into Aunt Kitty's car when Mr. Buckthorn's big, white SUV pulled in, followed by a silver sedan. Robin's dad and a man in a suit got out of the silver car. Right behind them came Charlie Bird's red pickup. Chase Fieldman and Sally were with him.

"Mr. Merriweather, Mr. Buckthorn," said Aunt Kitty. "How good to see you both."

Charlie helped Sally out of his truck. Chase was reaching for her chair when Sally waved him off. "I vill valk to the meeting. I vill stand on my own two feet and face the music."

"Miss Sonnschein," said Aunt Kitty. "The children and I have been out walking."

"You didn't see anymore shnakes, did you?" Sally asked, recoiling dramatically.

"Actually, Miss Sonnschein, we did," said Sierra, shrugging and holding up her camera. Chase stepped closer to see the snake photo. He played with his scruffy beard. "Hmm. That's very interesting," he said, studying the picture with a big smile.

"W-what? Who's a—what's a what?" asked a befuddled Mr. Buckthorn.

"This is a fox snake, Mr. Buckthorn. It's a highly unusual snake for this island. All recent reports indicate that Michigan's eastern fox snake, the *Elaphe vulpina,* is a state threatened and highly protected species." We all looked at each other.

I was confused. I thought Aunt Kitty said it was a western fox snake. But I kept my mouth shut, just in case she was wrong. Being wrong in front of lots of people can be embarrassing and I'd had enough of that recently.

"B-but it's a picture. How do we know it's this—this *laughing-pine* snake?" stammered Buckthorn.

"Look, Buckthorn, you can go ahead and purchase this property, but you won't be able to build your park if this land harbors a protected species," said Mr. Merriweather's lawyer. "Of course, you'll have to have a study done to see if the species in question is indeed the threatened or endangered snake. *If* they find it again, the snakes's DNA would have to be tested to determine that it is the protected specie. That could take months. What it all boils down to is, you should've done your homework. What is your decision, Mr. Buckthorn?"

"I-I…" Mr. Buckthorn stammered, throwing his hands up. "I have a boat to catch. H-here," he said pulling out the papers with Sally's signature. He ripped them in half. "And if you don't mind, I'd like my deposit back now, madam." Buckthorn's hand shot out.

Sally thumped her cane. "I don't have to give you your money back, Mr. Buckthorn. But if it means ve vill be rid of you, then here," she said, thrusting the check at him. Turning beet red, Buckthorn hustled back to his vehicle.

"I hope you enjoyed your stay, Mr. Buckthorn. Visit the island again," called Chase.

Buckthorn grumbled something and then stepped right smack into a fly-covered pile of Aunt Kitty's Green Bean-Pineapple-Sunrise-Surprise Salad.

"It's not called a Surprise Salad for nothing," snickered Aunt Kitty. The woman was wicked!

Buckthorn zoomed away from the lake. Chase and Aunt Kitty shook hands with Mr. Merriweather and his lawyer and walked them to their car.

"Vait! I vant a picture of you all," said Sally. "Ve vill all be in the newspaper next veek. 'Rescued Reptiles Rescue Beaver Island.'" Sierra snapped a picture of us.

"Eastern—western—we may never know for sure unless DNA testing is done, *if* we ever found this fella again," Chase said. "Besides, every snake needs a friend. And we really don't want a park here."

Aunt Kitty gave Chase a wink.

Sally laughed out loud and gave Charlie a high five, "Ve did it! You kids did it! I love shnakes!" Sally said, clapping. "And that's one shnake that vill never end up shtuffed in some museum."

"That was a close call," I said. "Just think, if I hadn't wanted to see a beaver so badly we might not have come back out here."

"And if Sie hadn't taken the picture for proof…" said T.

"And if T hadn't stood still, she would've scared the snake off," said Sie.

"Team Wild!" I yelled. "Robin, Sally, the fox snake of Fox Lake—we all saved the island!"

"All we have left is the art show and pet show judging," Gram said.

"The art show!" cried Sally. "I nearly forgot. Quickly people, moof, moof! Schnell! The judging is at three o'clock sharp."

"I'll get your collage from the hotel, girls," Aunty Kitty called as she dropped us off, her red kayak swinging wildly as her car turned the corner.

"It's 2:49. I hope she hurries," said Sie, nervously pushing up her glasses.

"If I know Kitty," said Gram, "she'll be here quicker than you can say 'porcupine.'"

Charlie's red truck rolled up to the school. "Out of the vay, people. Here comes the judge," announced Sally, parting the crowd.

"Let's look at the exhibit while we wait," said Gram.

Sally's new work hung at the entrance. People gathered around

gawking at her pieces. Her new painting titled *Extra Extravagant!* hung on an easel. It was Buckthorn's repainted sign from the lake! We saw Rusty's painted barn doors and old handsaws, Virginia's bird photos and lake sunsets, and even Charlie Bird had animal woodcarvings on display.

"It's 2:58," Sie poked me. I heard a familiar baying bark and a honk outside.

"See! I told you Kitty would make it!" I shouted as I ran to the curb. Hunter's big, slobbery head popped out the rear window.

"I brought Miss Tierra's pet portrait doll, also," said Aunt Kitty. She handed it to me through the front window.

An excited Hunter pranced in the rear as I opened the back door. I had just picked up Sierra's piece when Hunter scrambled into the rear seat.

"Huntie!" Aunt Kitty cried. But it was too late. He knocked me and the twins' art into a puddle of his drool. Oops! And eww! Times two.

The dog drool seemed to reactivate the glue. Dog hair, pine needles, cedar bits, Kenny's shed skin, sand—anything that had been in Aunt Kitty's car for the past three years was now plastered to the picture. Tierra's Willy/Wilma paper doll was now stuck smack in the middle of it all.

"Holy creeps, times ten." I knew the double twin trouble I'd be in.

"Hurry, Holly!" called Sierra from the door.

I rushed past both girls with the newly changed poster. Sierra's eyes popped as they zeroed in on the mess. I plopped it on the table by the tag *Beaver Island: A Living Museum by Sierra Hills.*

Next to Sierra's piece was Ivy Buckthorn's drawing of King

Strang. Naturally, Sally was judging this table first. I didn't have time to repair the damage.

"Holly H. Wild, what in the world happened to my piece?" Sie hissed. I turned to see the girls blur into one unhappy, angry friend. I cringed and smiled weakly.

"Junior Artist Category," Sally announced, holding a blue ribbon in her hand. "Who's verk is this? Explain please. Vat is this?" she asked, pointing at Ivy's art.

Ivy stepped forward, arms crossed. "That's King Strang. I wanted to portray a Beaver Island legend," she said smugly.

"Hhmpf, I see. I sought it vas an angry schicken," said Sally. "And this verk? Shtep up please. Quickly! Schnell!" ordered Sally.

Sierra pushed up her glasses and stepped forward.

"This verk," Sally pointed at Sierra's poster. "It's unbeliefable." Sally shook her head. "My child vat have you done?"

"Leave it to Stinkberry Shrimpcake's gang to come up with a mess like that," evil Ivy snickered.

"I don't know. It just—happened.'" Sierra said, glancing over at me.

"Precisely! That's how all art should be. It should just happen. I love collage. Such thought. Such placement, blending artifacts and history. Your photography, your textures, your fibers.

island art

Outshtanding verk! And I adore the little beaver sitting among the ferns."

"Uh, thank you?" said Sie, looking confused.

"Vat kind of glue did you use? It looks organic," asked Sally, studying it.

"Oh, trust me it is," I said.

"I guess you'd call it team work. We all had a hand in it," said Sie.

"And paw," I whispered.

"Marvelous!" declared Sally. "First place—Sierra Hills!" Sally slapped the ribbon onto the corner of Sie's art. "Such verk brings tears to my eyes. This piece truly captures Beaver Island life. Everysing is here." Sally bent over and whispered to Sierra. "May I purchase this for the museum?"

"Um, sure!" Sierra looked at T and me.

"Does a hundred dollars sound all right?" asked Sally.

"Um, yeah!" said Sierra. None of us

could believe our ears. I guess Ivy couldn't either, because she angrily stormed out of the school.

"Next category," called Sally, moving on.

Reporter Virginia Rail snapped our picture. "Congratulations!" she said shyly. "I'm glad life will get back to normal now. I can go back to shooting birds again. Click, shoot, with my camera. Not *boom,* shoot with a gun."

When we got outside Sie held up her ribbon and prize envelope. Aunt Kitty, Gram, Mom, Boy, and Robin started clapping.

"I told you everything would be OK," I said.

"Well, it did turn out—this time," said T.

"You and Hunter came up with a new art form. Drool-age," joked Sie.

"It'll be hard to go home after Museum Week. I love it here," said T.

"Fortunately, the island will stay this way for a long time," said Aunt Kitty. "People need a place to get away from the hustle-bustle of the busy world."

The *Emerald Isle* blasted its horn. We spotted the Buckthorns hurrying to the dock with their bags, dragging the yapping poodle and Ivy behind them.

"I guess Ivy's not staying for the pet show," said Sierra.

"Pet show? Kenny!" I slapped my forehead. "I forgot."

It was too late—the parade was already beginning. People lined the streets to watch. Rusty and Charlie sat on the Print Shop porch. "We're the judges this year," Rusty called.

"Sorry about your portrait of Willy—er Wilma, T," I said.

"Sorry Kenny missed the contest," T sighed. "On the bright side, Wilma's picture and Kenny's skin will always be in the art museum here."

"Yeah," I said, "Team Wild will be remembered on Beaver Island for a long time."

A little boy wearing a trout costume and carrying a goldfish bowl headed up the noisy parade, followed by kids dressed up as lions, cats, and growling bears. Then the pets and their owners marched past, spiffed up for judging. The last and smallest entrants, a pink stuffed bunny and a firefly in a jar that was decorated as the Beaver Island Harbor Lighthouse, were brought up to the porch and placed on the step.

The two judges smiled and whispered together.

First place went to the girl who had the firefly in a jar.

Virginia snapped the photo before the girl released the bottled bug. Then treats were handed out to dogs and owners alike.

"Good thing Hunter's not here, he'd have eaten all the cookies and had the toy bunny for dessert," said Tierra.

The horn blasted again as the boat left St. James Bay. Museum Week was officially over.

"This was a nice change, Mother Wild, but I'll be ready to go home tomorrow," Mom sighed. "It was fun, but my lazy days are over. I have a ton of laundry to do and the garden will need weeding and—the van! I hope it's still there." Mom was back to normal.

"Beaver Island is back to being an unspoiled, unhurried island," said Sie. "Case closed."

"*This* case. Now that I have a new poking stick, and the Scientific Method, just think of the places we can go," I said. "There are hundreds of wild places to visit, and we still have a bunch of summer vacation left. There's a lot more to explore!"

"I did have fun roughing it," said Tierra.

"I had a great time, too," said Sierra.

"My Michigan Indian legend book talks about huge sand dunes not far from here," I said. "Sleeping Bear Dunes National Lakeshore. It sounds like a cool place. There's a legend about a mother bear and her cubs. But she's sleeping now. How dangerous can a sleeping bear be anyway? It's only a legend, right?"

"Remember, sometimes stories—are not just stories," joked Sie, poking me in the ribs.

"It's funny you mention that, Holly, because that's where I'm headed next," said Aunt Kitty. "The park is having problems so I'm staying there for two weeks."

Hmm. To me that sounded like an invitation for Team Wild's help—times three!

Lori Taylor *is a Michigan author/artist/illustrator who has wandered the state's woods and waters on foot, bike, kayak, or canoe for stories ever since she was a child. She has been artist-in-residence for the Sleeping Bear Dunes National Lakeshore and the Porcupine Mountains Wilderness State Park.*

She taught her own kids and now her grandkids to "poke the world with a stick" and encourages others to do the same. Lori lives and works in Pinckney, MI with Kenny, Mr. Pickles (a new,old beagle), two cats, chickens and the editors of Bear Track Press. When Lori is not reading, writing, or drawing—she is sleeping!

To see Lori's art, books, photos, fun stuff and more visit:

www.loritaylorart.com

For information on Beaver Island's Museum Week Celebration, island history, nature and events, visit:

http://www.beaverisland.org/

HEY KIDS!
Join **TEAM WILD!**
and be a
GeEK!

Calling All Geo-Explorer Kids!

Michigan's herps (amphibians and reptiles) are important to the health of Michigan lakes, yards, and forests!

Water snakes and snapping turtles keep lakes free of decaying fish. Eastern massassaga rattlesnakes help control the rodent pest population, and their venom gives humans life-saving medicine.

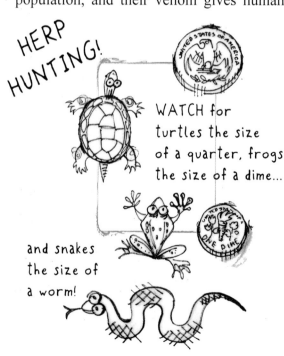

HERP HUNTING!

WATCH for turtles the size of a quarter, frogs the size of a dime...

and snakes the size of a worm!

Frogs and toads eat gazillions of garden pests and insects.

But right now Michigan herps are having a tough time. Herps are victims of habitat contamination and loss, acid rain, the illegal pet trade and roadkill!

**Here's how you can become a real GeEK
and lend a herp a helping hand!**

- Learn the songs of frogs and toads and be a citizen scientist and help count them on frog survey outings.
- Never hurt a herp! Amphibians and reptiles are living organisms and should be treated with care and respect.
- Handle herps gently and wear gloves. Did you know that lotions and bug sprays can harm frogs and snakes?
- Return herps to the place you found them. If you find a herp under an object, study it then place it **near** the replaced object so that it won't be crushed. Keep herp capture and study time short. Photos or sketches only.
- Don't leave garbage behind.
- Do not trespass! Ask permission before entering private land.
- Learn more about herps, especially Michigan's only venomous snake, the *eastern massasauga rattlesnake*. **DO NOT EVER DISTURB** this snake!

BEWARE and PROTECT!

LOOK and LISTEN for Michigan's only venomous snake. The Eastern Massasauga Rattlesnake likes wetland areas so watch your step!

Herps are secretive. Watching herps is like going birding. Learn the habits of the creatures you seek. Be in the right place at the right time. April to October is an active time of year for Michigan herps.

FOR MORE HERP INFO: Visit the Michigan Department of Natural Resources at: **www.michigan.gov/dnr**

Holly's
TIPS &
TOOLS

Holly Wild,
Hat Kid

"NO elf esteem"

"Take my tuk--
please!"

"NO magic here"

GET UP

10 gallon baby

"Big NO-NO
to Yo-ho-ho!"

GET UP

"Exploring hat"--just right!

Hats: collect berries, hold bones, protect your
head from the sun and hide freckles and gobs of
red hair.

HOLLY'S Mini-Explorer's kit

pen or pencil

"specimen" (pill) bottle

magnifying lens

flashlight

zipper lock bag

DATE:
"Field Notes"
Where?

'beaner

folded field note book

*Decorate and clip to your belt loop! EXPLORE!

Holly's "FIELD NOTE" Book.
(Or "Bird Fold" book)

1. Fold sheet of paper in half the long way.

2. Fold in half again. It should look like the letter V.

COVER

3. Fold left and right sides down to center fold. Now it looks like a sea gull or the letter M.

Easy times two and good for sketching, notes and holds leaves, tiny shells, or sand samples inside. Now you're ready to explore!

Holly's
TRACK RULER

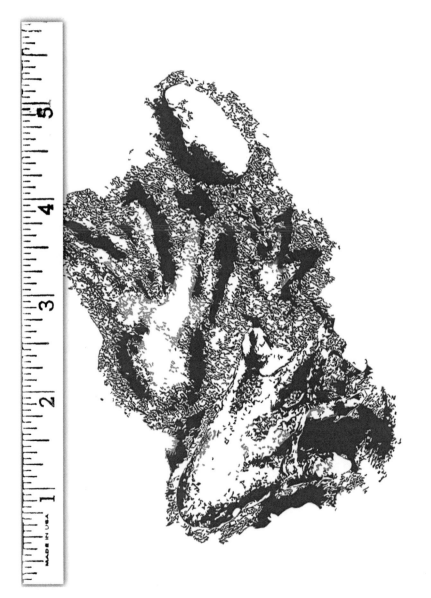

FIELD Note Books are for:

- recording place and date
- time of day and weather
- taking secret notes
- taping in special items

gull
feather

from the
day Ivy
got pooped on

Sie's
WEATHER PAGES

A few pages from Sie's Weather Book about the **Beaufort Weather Scale of Wind and Weather.**

calm   0-1 mph
(smoke rises vertically)

light air   1-3
(smoke drifts slowly)

slight breeze   4-7
(leaves rustle)

gentle breeze   8-12
(leaves/twigs in motion)

moderate breeze   13-18
(small branches move)

fresh breeze   19-24
(small trees sway)

DRAW the weather where you are!

Mon.   Tues.   Wed.

Thurs.   Fri.   Sat.

Sun.

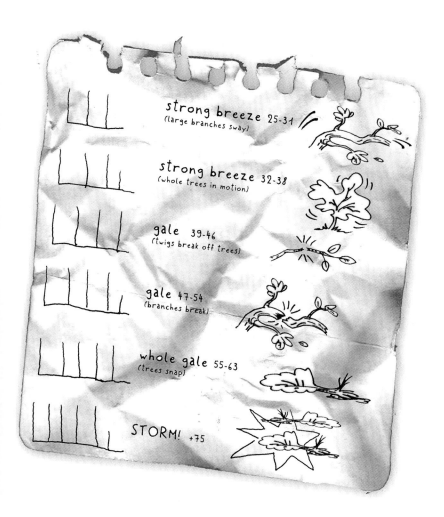

Aunt kitty's
TIC-TRACK-TOE!

FIND three rodent family tracks in a row and you win!

LABEL the tracks of deer, mink, cat, chipmunk, squirrel, dog porcupine, beaver and muskrat.

WHICH animal is RUNNING SOUTH? WHICH animal is traveling WEST? WHICH animal is heading EAST?

Tierra's
ART TIPS

With a glitter pen or glitter crayon,
COLOR in the snakes in Chapter 21
for your very own handy snake guide.
Color HINTS:

yellow stripes - Garter Snake
lime green - Green Snake
tan with brown blotches - Fox Snake
dark blue w/ orange-neck ring - Ring-necked Snake
tan with red-orange belly - Red-bellied Snake
brown or gray - Northern Water Snake
tan with red-brown blotches - Milk Snake

YOUR OWN
GeEK NOTES:

GeEK Motto: "There's always more to EXPLORE!"

OTHER TITLES BY LORI TAYLOR

Holly Wild: Bamboozled on Beaver Island (Book 1)
Holly Wild: Let Sleeping Bear Dunes Lie (Book 2)
Holly Wild: Packing For the Porkies! (Book 3)
Holly Wild: Questpedition for da Yooper Stone (Book 4)

Lissy-Lost!

GRAPHIC READERS

Crazy Cat Don't Chase That Rabbit
Hot Times in the Big Creek Wood

157

JOIN THE HOLLY WILD GEO-EXPLORER KID TEAM!

BAMBOOZLED on BeaVeR iSLANd

HOLLY WILD

written & illustrated by LORI TAYLOR

ONLY
$12.99

BE A GEEK!
(GEO-EXPLORER KID)

Get INTO crazy wild adventure with HOLLY WILD
A super fun, super Michigan middle-grade nature
mystery series for kids 7-12!

* wacky science
* weird nature
* fun games and
  lotsa, LOTSA
  art inside!

Packing for the PORKIES!

HOLLY WILD

written & illustrated by LORI T...

ORDER YOURS TODAY!
WWW.LORITAYLORART.COM

158